Stafford Family Summer

Glenna Guffey

God Bless!
Love you later!
Glenna

PublishAmerica
Baltimore

ISBN: 978-1-4489-6106-1
PUBLISHED BY PUBLISHAMERICA, LLLP
www.publishamerica.com
Baltimore

Printed in the United States of America

Dedication

I would like to thank God for giving me the inspiration and the ability to write this. I would like to dedicate this book to my daughters, Katie and Rachel, who mean the world to me. I would also like to dedicate it to Katie's fifth grade teacher, Mrs. Wanda Phillips, and the whole fifth grade class. Without whose encouragement and interest I would not have been able to get this finished.

Chapter 1

It was a very hot and humid late spring day. I was watching the dust fly from underneath the bus. It was the last day of school for this year. I didn't know if Mama would be happy or mad when she sees my report card. After all I did pass, but just barely. My name is Alexis Renea Stafford. Alex for short. From my vantage point in the back of the bus, I can see all the other kids from the community where I live. It's a small out of the way dot on the bigger map of Tennessee. We live in the country. Some people call it the boonies. We are also referred to as hillbillies. Either way, it's a good place to live. I have lived here all my life. All eleven, almost twelve, years. Everyone else is kind of rowdy. I guess they are happy to be out of school. Don't get me wrong, I'm happy too but I'm just not the rowdy type. There's no sense in it.

My sisters, Olivia and Isabelle, are sitting toward the middle of the bus surrounded by their friends. They seem to be talking all at once. I don't see how they can understand each other. It just reminds me of a bunch of chickens all cackling at once. I'm not much of a people person. I prefer the smell of the barn and the company of animals,they don't care what I'm wearing or whether I even brush my hair. They accept me for who I am. I don't have to worry about impressing them with my wit or my clothes.

The bus stops to let the Smith kids off. There's five of them; three boys and two girls. They are all laughing and picking on each other as they get off the bus. There is a small pond in the field on my side of the bus. I notice a long legged crane standing at the edge and gazing intently into the water. He's probably waiting for a fish or a bug or something. We start to pull away and someone slides into the seat beside me and grabs my arm.

"Whatcha looking at?" It's Bobby Hall, my nearest neighbor and my best friend.

"Nuthin." I really don't want to talk right now.

"Ain't you glad to be out of school?" he asks.

"I guess." I mumble.

"Whatcha going to do this summer?" He says, determined to make me talk.

"I don't really know yet. It just depends." I hope he doesn't ask anything else about what I'm going to do. I hate to have to tell him that I won't be doing anything or going anywhere.

"I'm going to Kentucky to see my grandma." He flashes a smile, showing his white teeth in his freckled face. The bus hits a bump and his red curls bounce all over his head.

"That sounds nice." I can't help but smile. His enthusiasm is infectious. He is always able to make me laugh and he always seems to find the good in everything. We have been friends ever since before we could both walk.

"I don't get to see them very much. It's fun going to visit. They always have so much for me to do and Grandma makes the best chocolate chip cookies in the world!"

"When are you going?" I want to know.

"I'm not sure yet, probably when Daddy gets some time off work. He's been working a lot of overtime lately." He's got the perfect family. His Dad works at a factory in town. They make some kind of car part. I'm not sure what, exactly. His Mama stays home and takes care of his little brother, Carl. Carl was born with a birth defect. The Doctors say he is Autistic.

"I hope you're around some. I've got to have someone to talk to besides my sisters. They make me crazy!! All they want to do is listen to their music and giggle about boys!" I just don't think I could stand that for the whole summer.

"Don't worry, I'll be around." That is a good thing.

The bus pulls up the hill to Bobby's house. It's a pretty place with a white fence around the yard. Carl is sitting in the tire swing in the big oak tree in the front of the house. He spots the bus and starts waving and yelling. He jumps out of the swing and runs toward the gate. He stops short at the gate because he can't open it. Howard, the bus driver, stops and opens the door and tells Bobby to be good and have a good summer. Carl is bouncing up and down, clapping and smiling from ear to ear. He really loves Bobby. "Bobby, Bobby!" he chants over and over. Bobby turns and waves as the bus pulls away. I wave back. Carl hugs him as he goes through the gate.

Looking straight ahead, I watch as the bus chugs slowly toward our house. We come the top of a small hill and I can see the roof of our old farmhouse. It's not much but it's home. As we start down the other side of the hill, the view of the house gets clearer. The yard is small, with a bare spot under the tire swing in the big tree. Most people around here have a tire swing in their yard. That's a big thing. Rufus, our dog, runs to the edge of the driveway, waiting for the bus. Rufus is a mutt. He's about knee high with long ears and big brown eyes. He is red with a hint of brindle. He's some kind of hunting dog. He just showed up here one day and he's been here ever since. I guess he just adopted us. He's wagging his tail excitedly. The bus pulls around the circular drive. We are the last house on this road, It's a dead end road. Howard tells us all to have a great summer and he'll see us later. After he closes the door, he pulls away, the gravel crunching under the tires.

Daddy is sitting on the porch in a rocking chair with his head laid back and his eyes closed. He's still wearing the same clothes he had on yesterday, probably didn't bother to change. He looks up as we walk into the yard. "Howdy, girls. How was school today?" he asks after he spits tobacco juice over the porch railing.

"Okay, Daddy. Are you feeling well today?" asks Olivia.

"Okay. My back is killing me and I've got a headache." He's always got something wrong or hurting. I have never seen him completely okay.

'Where's Mama?" I ask.

"She'll be back in a little bit. She went to clean Mrs. Buckner's house. She always pays good." Mama was always cleaning or doing something to make some extra money.

"I thought you had a job today." Isabelle said with a frown.

"I did. I went and cut down that big tree in Hollis' yard and he paid me. My back got to hurting so bad I came home and sat here."

"I'm sorry you're hurting, Daddy." Isabelle says. "Did you get paid for the job today?"

"Yes, I did. It was just $50.00. It's all got to go on bills, though."

"All of it?" she asks. She was looking forward to getting this little blue dress she has spotted at the thrift shop in town.

"Yes, all of it." He closes his eyes and lays his head back in the chair.

I open the front door and go into the house. The screen door slams shut behind me. I go into the kitchen and open the refrigerator to get some water. The light doesn't come on. I flip the light switch on the wall and nothing. I guess they pulled the meter today because the bill hasn't been paid. It's not the first time. The electric company won't give a person a chance any more.

"What happened to the lights? I can't listen to my radio!" Olivia yells from her room upstairs. She thinks she would die without her radio.

"The electric bill didn't get paid and they turned our lights off." I yell back at her.

"I can't see in the bathroom!" Isabelle yells. Like that is a major catastrophe!

"Don't know. Couldn't tell ya!" I yell back.

I go to my room and put my backpack on the bed. I quickly put on my old clothes. It's time for my favorite part of the day. Star, our horse, gets my full attention for a while. He is solid black with a white star shaped mark on his face, that's where he gets his name. I look out the window and he's standing at the barn waiting for me. I slip on my old barn shoes and head out. He whinnies when he sees me coming down the path to the barn. He knows who feeds him and he's just telling me it's feeding time.

"Be careful out there!" Daddy yells from the front porch. He hasn't moved. He's still sitting in the same position with his head laid back. The walk to the barn is not very long. It only takes a couple of minutes. The feed room door is already open. Star's bucket is laying on the floor. Someone's been in here. I put it on the nail where it goes after I fed last night. About that time, Puss jumps out of the rafters and lands on the floor in front of me. She looks up at me and says "meow."

"You scared me, puss! Did you make this mess?" She just purrs and rubs against my legs, as if to say "I'm sorry."

I put a couple scoops of feed in the bucket. Star hears me and stands at his feed trough, waiting patiently. I grab his brush as I go out the door. It takes a few minutes to brush him and he holds very still. I think he likes it. After I get through with the brush, I pour his feed in the trough where he can get it. He munches loudly on the pieces of corn. The chickens are next. There's just a few but we still get plenty of eggs. There's just eight tonight. That's enough for our breakfast in the morning. Mama says that when the young ones start laying, we can sell more eggs.

On my way back to the house, Mama pulls up in the old truck. I can hear it coming for quite a ways. It sounds kind of like one of those race cars. As she opens the door to get out, I can tell she's tired by the way she moves. She pauses with one foot out the door and just sits there with her head in her hands. It must have been a good minute or two. She looks up and sees me watching her and she quickly straightens up and gets out of the truck. She smiles and waves.

"Come here, Alex, I've got some things I need help with." She motions for me to come to her.

"I'm coming, Mama!" When I get to the truck, I can see some boxes of stuff on the passenger side seat. I also catch a whiff of something that smells heavenly. Pizza. I love pizza. Mama must have seen the expression on my face.

"Mrs. Buckner sent some pizzas for you girls for supper. She knows how much you like them." Mrs. Buckner is a small, frail, old lady who lives down the road about five miles or so. Her husband died last year of cancer. She can't take care of herself very much so she hired Mama to help her. I go with her a lot and help too. She always pays me a little extra when I come to help. So far, I've got $25.00 saved and put away so that nobody knows where it is or that I've even got it.

"Mama, I've got some money saved up if you want it I guess you know we don't have any electricity." I offer as we get the boxes out of the truck. I can see that they are full of groceries like canned stuff and things that won't ruin.

"No that's all right. That's your money. You might need something or see something you really want. You earned it yourself. Anyway, I made enough the last few days to pay the electric bill. I just couldn't get to town today to get it paid. Your Daddy was gone most of the day then I had to go to Mrs. Buckner's. I think your Daddy has some to put in, too." I don't know how she does it. Since Daddy got hurt, she has been paying all the bills. That's been a long time now. She doesn't want to go to work in a factory because of us. She wants to be able to be there for us if we need her. She tells everyone that it is her responsibility to raise her girls, not someone else's.

We carry the boxes into the kitchen. Daddy comes in as we are putting them all away.

"What did you get today?" he asks. "I'm hungry. I ain't eat nothin since this morning."

"Mrs. Buckner sent some pizzas. I'm glad because I really don't feel like building a fire in that old cook stove just to cook some supper. I am tired and hot." We have an old fashioned wood cook stove under a shed behind the house. It used to be my Grandmother's. Mama uses it a lot in the summer for canning. She says it doesn't heat the house up that way. She cooks on it a lot, too. When it gets bad in the winter time, the electric goes off because some of the power lines get knocked down. So its not like we're not used to doing without electric.

"Mama, when are you going to get the electric back on again?" Olivia asks as she comes into the room. Not a hello Mom or anything.

"I guess we'll have to wait till Monday, now. The office is already closed and they're not open on Saturday." Mama says as she hands her some groceries to put up. "We'll be okay till then, At least it's warm weather and it's not snowing! It could be a whole lot worse." Mama always tries to look at the bright side of things. She's always saying a positive attitude is the best thing to have.

"Oh, yummy! I smell pizza!" Isabelle says as she enters the kitchen.

"Slow down there, there's plenty for everyone!" Mama gives her a quick hug.

After all the groceries are put away, we open the pizza boxes. The aroma fills the whole room. Mama gets the paper plates out of the cabinet. Olivia and Isabelle are waiting to grab a piece and Daddy is already sitting in his usual chair.

"Dang it! You know I don't like this kind!" He bellows, kind of hateful. "Why can't you get what I like?"

"Beggars can't be choosey! It was give to me, so eat it and be grateful you have it!" Mama gives him a dirty look out of the corner of her eye.

The pizza is really good. We don't get store bought ones very often, so when we do it's a treat. Don't get me wrong, Mama makes them a lot and hers are really good too but it's nice getting one that someone else has made. It must be the different taste.

"When you girls get through, claan up your mess." Mama reminds us.

"Fix me a plate, I'm going back to the porch. Be sure you bring me something to drink!" Daddy pushes his chair back from the table and gets up slowly. He walks back to the porch with a very pronounced limp. Mama fixes a plate for him and gets a glass of water.

"I'll take it to him. I know you're tired." I offer.

She looks at me and smiles. She reaches over and hugs me and whispers "You're a good kid! I am really blessed to have you and your sisters! I thank God for you all every day!" She always has a way of making us feel wanted and loved and appreciated no matter what else is going on around us.

When I get to the porch with the Daddy's supper, he's sitting with his feet propped up on the railing, looking out at the woods on the other side of the driveway.

"What took you so long?" he asks. He must have been expecting Mama because when he turned and saw it was me, he looked surprised. "Where's your Mama?"

"She's still in the kitchen." I answer, handing him the plate and water. He sits the plate on his lap and the water on the porch beside his chair.

"Tell her I said to come here." he orders after spitting his chew of tobacco into his hand and tossing it in the yard. That makes Mama mad because somebody usually ends up stepping in it and tracking it in the house. It's usually Daddy, too. You would think that since he threw it out there he would know it's there and avoid stepping in it. When I get back to the kitchen, Mama is eating a slice of pizza and talking to my sisters.

"Did you girls get your report cards today?"

"Yea, mine is really good! I got all A's and B's and I'll be a Junior next year! Just two more years to go and I'm out of school." Olivia says. She is really looking forward to being out of school.

"Mine is okay. I've got one C and the rest are A's and B's." Isabelle sounds pretty proud of herself. "I'll be in High School next year! I can't wait to get there. It's going to be so much fun." Mama looks at me, waiting for me to say something. I just don't want to make her mad.

"Daddy says for you to come there. He wants to talk to you." I'm trying to change the subject so she doesn't ask me again. I pick up a slice of pizza and take a bite.

"Laura, I said to come here!" Daddy yells from the front porch. She sighs and puts her pizza on the paper plate sitting in front of her and stands, pushing her chair back. She walks toward the porch.

"Why didn't you tell her about your grades?" Olivia asks.

"Well," I swallow the bite of pizza I have in my mouth. "I just don't want to upset her. She's got enough to worry about right now."

Mama comes back into the kitchen. She doesn't say anything. She picks up the empty boxes and turns to take them to the garbage on the back porch. Her eyes look a little red and watery like she might start crying at any minute. She lowers her head and goes to the back porch, putting the boxes in the garbage and putting the lid back on it She stands and gazes out at the chicken coop with her back to the house. She raises her hand to her face, like she is wiping away tears. It takes a lot to make Mama cry. I guess Daddy is not giving her any money again. Just then, the truck starts up and pulls out. Mama waits for a minute and then turns around to come back into the house. "Did you girls feed all the animals?" she asks, trying not to let us see her face,

"I did, Mama. I also gathered the eggs. They're sitting on the counter beside the fridge." I tell her.

"Thank you, Alex. I really appreciate it. Can you girls get the clothes off the line? I'm glad I got them all done before they pulled the meter," she asks Olivia and Isabelle:

"Sure. We'll fold them and put them up, too." Isabelle offers. They both head out the door, stopping to get the clothes basket where it sits on the porch beside the door. There is a heavy silence for a few minutes. I don't know what to say to help Mama. I know she's upset.

"You never did tell me about your report card. Did you pass?"

"Yea, I passed." I answer quietly, barely above a whisper.

"You don't sound very enthused about it. What were your grades?" This is the moment I have been dreading. I just wish I could disappear.

"Well, they're not that bad."

"Tell me. I don't bite."

"Okay, I got one B, a couple of C's and one D." I brace myself for the disappointment in her voice.

"Did you really try, or were you just playing around?"

"I really tried. I'm just not any good at math. I don't understand it."

"That's okay. You can do it. You are a smart girl. You just have to apply yourself a little more. Some people get it the first time they do it and some have to do it several times. You just need to study a little more." She takes my chin in her hand and lifts my face so I have to look at her. I look into her green eyes and see the love there. I shouldn't have been worried at all.

"Okay, Mama. I'll try harder next year. I promise I will study more." I give her a big hug. "I love you." I just don't know what I would do without Mama.

"I love you too." she replies with a big smile.

Olivia and Isabelle come back into the house with a basket full of clothes. They're both laughing about something.

"What's so funny?" Mama asks "Share it, we could all use a good laugh."

"We were talking about what happened at school in the cafeteria today." Isabelle explains. "It was so funny'."

"Frank Walton was walking to put his tray up after he finished eating. Somebody had spilled some mashed potatoes on the floor and he stepped right in them. The next thing we know, he's on the floor on his butt, covered with what's left of his lunch." Olivia laughs. Frank Walton is the local jock, I mean jerk. He comes from a rich family and thinks he's all that and then some. All the girls go nuts over him. He's a Sophomore, so he's got several years of football and basketball and being big man on campus ahead of him. Personally, I think it all goes to his head.

"I bet that was funny! I would have liked to have seen that" I meant it, too. It's always nice to see someone like that get what's coming to them. Mama kind of laughed, too.

"Now girls, how would you feel if that had been you?"

"Not very good." Isabelle says.

"Me either." Olivia adds after much thought. As usual, Mama is right.

"Well, girls, let's get these clothes folded and put away. It won't take long with all of us working at it. It'll be dark before long and then we won't be able to see very well." She picks up the basket and sits it on the kitchen table. It doesn't take long to fold them all. We each take a pile to put up. By this time, it's starting to get dark. We all go to the front porch and sit in the rocking chairs. Nobody mentions Daddy. He'll come back when he gets ready to. He always does.

The sound of frogs croaking fills the night air. There is a slight breeze blowing, carrying with it the smell of honeysuckle. Mama smiles and lays her head back and shuts her eyes. She looks so peaceful. Gradually, the night sounds fill the air. A feeling of complete peace settles over us. It's such a wonderful feeling and noone wants to say anything to spoil the moment. This makes you realize just how big and wonderful God is. It gets your priorities straight and we realize just how blessed we really are. Just think, the people with electricity are probably sitting in their living rooms watching tv and missing out on all this! I kind of feel sorry for them.

"Girls, I think it's about bedtime, don't you?" Mama finally breaks the silence. We all agree and make our way to our rooms. The last thing I remember is listening to the frogs.

Chapter 2

The rooster crowing wakes me up. The sun is shining and the smell of wood smoke floats through my window. Mama must be fixing breakfast. Olivia and Isabelle are coming down the stairs. They are arguing about something but I can't tell what it is. There is no telling with them.

"Alex, it's time to get up!" Mama calls from the kitchen. The smell of bacon makes my stomach growl. I roll out of bed and stretch. The birds are singing outside and somewhere in the distance Rufus is barking. He's probably got a rabbit or something. Rummaging through my closet, I find a pair of old shorts and an old t-shirt. Mama would skin me if I put on my good clothes to work around here. I don't remember hearing Daddy come home last night. He stays gone all night sometimes. I don't know where he goes, but he eventually comes back. On my way to the kitchen, I pass Mama's room and the door is closed so I guess he came home. He'll probably sleep most of the day and won't want to be disturbed. The kitchen smells heavenly. There's eggs, biscuits, and gravy to go with the bacon I smell. Mama sure is a good cook. Even without electricity, she can fix a meal that any fancy chef would envy. There are a couple of big coolers on the floor in front of the fridge. I guess Daddy brought home some ice for all the cold stuff. We use these coolers a lot. Mama opens one and gets out a jug of milk. She reaches for a glass and pours some and hands it to me.

"Good morning, sleepyhead!" She says. I walk over and give her a hug. She says the first hug in the morning is always the best.

"Good morning!" I take the glass from her and pull out the chair and sit down at my usual spot at the table. "Could you pass the bacon, please?" I ask Isabelle. She hands me the platter. "Thank you!"

"When we get finished with breakfast, the dishes need to be done and the animals at the barn need to be taken care of. When all that is done, we are going to work in the garden. It's supposed to rain this afternoon and we need to get the garden worked." Mama informs us.

"Yes, Maam." we all say in unison. The garden is our lifeline. Mama cans the most of it and the extra she sells. With the money she gets from the garden, she buys our school clothes. It really makes a difference.

"Is there hot water on the stove?" Isabelle asks. The well pump won't work without electric, so we have to use the old well bucket to get water out of the well. Olivia and Isabelle quickly finish eating and get up to start the dishes. They don't like going to the barn, so they think they are pulling one over on me by fixing it so that I have to go to the barn and feed the animals. I let them think that. I would rather do that than dishes, any day.

After eating, I go out on the back porch and get the milk bucket. It's laying upside down on a clean towel on the table, it's usual spot. Daddy milks through the week because we have to be on the bus for school by 6:00. It's quite a ways to school and there are a lot of other stops to make. I head for the barn, bucket in hand. The chickens are all running around and chasing bugs and such. Star whinnies as if to say "Good morning." I know he's probably wanting to be fed but he only gets feed in the evening now because the grass is good and green. Old Bessie, the milk cow, is waiting patiently in her stall. She's got the routine down pat. I stop by the feed room and get a scoop of grain for her. She quickly starts chowing down. By the time I'm through milking, she has the trough licked clean. We've had her for several years now. The other cow is expecting a calf and it shouldn't be much longer till she has it.

With the bucket full of white frothy milk I head back to the house. As I walk into the kitchen, I notice that Daddy is up and sitting at the table eating his breakfast. No one is saying anything. We know better. We don't dare talk to him or make any sounds when he first gets up because if we do, we are in trouble. Olivia and Isabelle are quietly doing dishes. Mama takes the bucket of milk and starts straining it. She pours it through a thin piece of material to get the impurities out of it. When she finishes, she pours it into a glass gallon jug and puts a lid on it and leaves it sitting out on the counter to clabber to make butter and buttermilk. She has an old fashioned churn that belonged to my grandma and we use it all the time. What we have extra, Mama sells. There are a lot of people that buy butter from her.

"Well, girls, I see you all are getting with it this morning. That's good. I hope you all are going to work in the garden today. It needs it." Daddy says after he scoots the chair back from the table.

"Jim, are you going to help us?" Mama asks.

"My back is hurting this morning. I think I will go lay back down for a while. Try to be quiet so I can sleep." Sometimes I wonder if he is really hurting or if it's just an excuse to get out of helping with the chores. I know I shouldn't think like that, after all he is my daddy and we were always taught to respect our elders. I don't mean to sound disrespectful. Sometimes I do wonder, though.

"Mama, are we going to get started on the garden right now? It would be better now before it gets hot" Isabelle asks.

"Yes, just as soon as we can." Mama answers.

The garden is pretty good sized. It'll take a while to get it all worked out. There is a little bit of everything in it. Corn, beans, potatoes, okra, tomatoes. and several other things. The plants are all up about three or four inches. They are looking good right now. I sure hope it all does okay. We all get to work. Hoeing and weeding. Mama starts the tiller and goes between the rows to get the ground loose and the weeds gone. Time passes pretty quickly. It's about lunch time when we finish the last row. It's getting very hot and muggy. There are several clouds already gathering in the distance. Every now and then, we hear a very faint clap of thunder.

"Looks like we're getting done about the right time." mama comments, looking at the sky. We put the hoes back into the shed and head toward the house. There is a bucket sitting on the table beside the well. Mama gets some fresh water out of the well and pours it into the bucket. We take turns drinking out of a dipper that hangs on the wall on a nail for that purpose. The water is ice cold and tastes really good about now. Mama says there are springs feeding our well and that's what makes it cold because the water is moving under the ground all the time. "Do you all want some lunch? There is some lunch meat for sandwiches and I got you all a drink." Mama doesn't allow us to have drinks very much. She says they're not good for you to have all the time.

Olivia and Isabelle go into the kitchen and start taking sandwich fixings out of the coolers and sitting it on the table.

"Did you get any chips to go with them?" Olivia asks.

"Yes. Look on top of the refrigerator." Mama tells her. She doesn't allow us to have chips very often either. While we're eating, the thunder is getting closer and closer. There is a very deep rumble. "Sounds like the storm is getting closer. When you're finished eating, don't you think it might be a good idea to feed Star and take care of the chickens before it starts to rain?" she asks because it might be raining at feeding time.

"We'll clean up the kitchen." Olivia offers.

After I finish my sandwich and gulp down the last sip of Dr. Pepper, I head out the door. The sky looks very menacing in the distance. It's going to come a pretty good storm. Rufus is sitting on the back porch and he jumps up and wags his tail as I come out the door. "Hey, boy, do you want to come to the barn with me to take care of everything?" He just wags his tail even harder and wiggles all over. I scratch behind his ears and we walk to the barn. As I approach the feed room door, Puss is coming out. She stops in her tracks as she spots Rufus. She glares at him and takes off up the ladder to the hay loft. Rufus looks kind of hurt and lays down at the bottom of the ladder. They are usually pretty good buddies. "It's okay, boy. You know how cats are. They get moody and anti-social sometimes."

I feed Star and put the bucket back into the room. I can hear the thunder getting closer and closer. The wind has picked up and is blowing through the hallway of the barn causing the loose hay and dust to swirl around, making me squint my eyes to keep them from getting filled with dust. Rufus is pacing back and forth, nervously looking at me then toward the house. I quickly feed the chickens and gather the eggs. Rufus runs ahead of me toward the house, pausing every few feet to turn and make sure I am still following him. When we reach the house, he jumps on the back porch and curls up next to the door. He would go in the house if we would let him. He hates storms, especially after the bad one that came through here a couple of years ago that blew trees over and it hailed so much that it broke just about all the windows out. There were piles of ice laying in the yard for several hours after it quit. Some of the woods looked like those pictures you see about countries that have been bombed. It was very scary for everyone. The news said it was just straight line winds and not a tornado. Just as I get to the steps, the rain starts falling. I stop and turn my face up to the sky, letting the raindrops run down my face.

"Are you going to come in out of the rain?" Mama asks from the back door.

"I guess I had better!" I tell her just as a streak of lightning lights up the sky. I sit the eggs on the counter and grab a towel that's laying on the table and wipe my face. I've got to admit, the rain felt pretty good. There is a roar all through the house as the rain comes down hard on the tin roof. After a minute, It lessens some and it's just a steady sound. I love summer storms like this. It's just so relaxing. Olivia is sitting on the couch on the phone. I'm surprised Mama lets her talk with a storm outside. She is giggling at something the other person is saying. Isabelle is sitting in the chair with a book in her hands. I go to my bedroom and shut the door. A good book sounds like a good idea. There's nothing else to do right now. After changing into dry clothes and hanging my wet ones on the back of the chair sitting at my desk, I grab the Nancy Drew book I have been reading. Mama gave me her collection she had when she was a little girl. They are very good books. After an hour or two, I'm not sure how long, the rain finally stops. Isabelle comes to the door.

"What ya reading?" she inquires.

"Nancy Drew."

"How can you stand to read that stuff? Give me a good romance any day."

"I would rather figure out who did it and why. It keeps my mind active." I really don't like romance and all that mushy stuff. I would rather have something that I have to figure out.

"Okay. Olivia and I were wondering about something. We know that Mrs. Buckner pays you extra when you go help Mama at her house.

Anyway, we were wondering if we could have $20.00 at least to get some batteries for our radio. Daddy said he would go get them if we could get him some gas money, too."

"Oh, did he finally get up?"

"Yea. He got up and ate some supper. He's sitting on the porch waiting for the money."

"What makes you think I have any money at all?"

"I don't know for sure but we do know you get paid for helping Mama and you don't ever spend any money on anything that we know of. We just figured you've got plenty of money put up." Isabelle looks at the floor and waits for an answer.

"I don't have any extra money right now. I'm sorry, if I had some, I would help pay the electric bill and get our lights back on."

"I guess that makes a lot of sense." She looks kind of disappointed. I think Daddy is just wanting some money to go running around on and he's trying to play on Olivia and Isabelle's sympathy. Again, I am not supposed to be disrespectful, but that's what I think.

"Isabelle, come back here. I need to talk to you." Daddy yells from the porch. She gives me this please help look and turns around and walks slowly to the front door. I feel for her. I hope Daddy doesn't get mad and fuss at her too much. She doesn't do well with fussing. I get back to reading my book. It's getting really good.

It's starting to get dark, I can barely see to read anymore. I can hear Mama in the kitchen. I guess I'll go see what she's doing and see if I can help do anything. She is sitting at the kitchen table going through some quilting patterns. She looks up as I come into the room. "Hi, did you get your book finished?"

"No. It got too dark. I'm almost done with it though. It's getting to the best part now. What are you doing?" I ask, going to the counter beside the sink and getting a glass of water.

"I'm just going through some old patterns I have. Mrs. Thompson is wanting to buy a quilt for her mother for Christmas and I thought I would get started on it early. What do you think she would like?"

"I don't know. You know more about that than I do."

"I know she likes sunflowers. I've got a pattern for one here somewhere."

"Where's Daddy and Olivia and Isabelle?"

"I guess they're all in their rooms. Your Daddy went back to bed, he said he was still tired. His back was hurting, too."

"Okay, I was just wondering. I knew I didn't hear the truck leave."

"Would you like something to eat? There's still some sandwich meat left from lunch. I think there may still be some chips too."

"No, thank you. I'm really not hungry right now." Mama got up and lit the coal oil lamp sitting on the table so we could see. The flame flickered and sent shadows dancing all around the room. It was really nice and peaceful. Outside, the frogs were really croaking. They love this rain. It had cooled down a lot. "Why don't we go sit on the porch where it's good and cool?"

"That's a good idea." Mama picks up the lamp and carries it in front of us as we go to the porch. She sits it on a small table that sits beside the front door. The night air feels really good and we sit in the rocking chairs. The only sounds are the frogs and the rocking chairs making little squeaking noises as we rock back and forth. It is a comfortable silence. I yawn and stretch after a while.

"I guess I'll go to bed now. I love you Mama." I stand up and lean over and kiss her on the cheek.

"I love you too, baby. Good night and I will see you in the morning. I think I'll just sit here for a while." As I go to my room, the sound of the chair rocking back and forth makes a steady lullaby to help me fall asleep.

Chapter 3

The morning sun wakes me up. the birds are singing outside my window and there is a cool breeze blowing my curtains just a little. Today is Sunday. I can already smell the sausage cooking on the stove. Mama always makes pancakes and sausage on Sunday. We finally got the electricity back on last Tuesday. I wouldn't miss it myself, but my sisters would both die of boredom! I pick out my favorite dress and lay it across the foot of my bed. Today is a special day because it's homecoming at church. We have a singing, preaching, dinner on the grounds, more singing and more preaching. Mama baked several pies last night. She was going to fry some chicken and make some potato salad. There are a lot of good cooks there.

"Alex, are you up yet?" Mama yells from the kitchen.

"Yea, I'm up. I'll be in there in just a minute." I've got to go do my chores before breakfast. It may be Sunday but the animals still need to be fed and taken care of. I go through the kitchen and Olivia and Isabelle are helping Mama with breakfast.

"Boy, something sure smells good!!" Daddy says as he comes into the room from outside. He's got a bucket of white, frothy milk. "Alex, you don't have to do your chores, I've already done them for you."

"Thank you! I appreciate that'." I don't know what got into him today. I'm not going to complain, though.

"Jim, sit that bucket on the counter by the sink and wash your hands for breakfast." Mama tells him. He sits the bucket down and turns on the faucet, washing his hands. Everyone sits down to eat.

"Are you all going to church?" Daddy asks.

"Yea, we always go to Homecoming. Why don't you go with us?" Mama tells him.

"Yea, please go with us Daddy." Olivia and Isabelle chime in togethor.

"No, I guess I'll stay here. I just don't feel like going anywhere. My back is killing me. I think I will take it easy today." He used to go with us to Church. I don't know what happened, he just quit going one day. I wish he would go.

"It's going to be kind of later this afternoon when we get back home." Mama tells him. "Do you want me to bring you a plate?"

"Yea, just bring me a plate."

After we are finished eating and the kitchen is cleaned up, Olivia and Isabelle are fighting over who gets the bathroom first. Mama is playing referee while she is trying to get the food ready to take. Daddy goes to the porch and sits in his rocking chair with his feet propped up on the railing and Rufus is laying beside him. He lays his head back and closes his eyes. After I finish getting ready, I walk out to the porch and sit down beside Daddy to wait for Mama, Olivia, and Isabelle. For a little while, there is complete silence and I'm beginning to think that he's asleep.

"Are you ready to go?" he asks me without opening his eyes.

"Yea. I thought you were asleep. Why don't you get ready and go with us? I would really like for you to go."

"I just don't feel like going. I'll just stick around here and maybe take a nap after while." He answers me, still with his eyes closed.

"It would be really nice to have you there. You used to go with us, what happened?"

"Let's just say some people aren't what they seem to be and leave it at that."

"But there has to be a better reason. Please tell me what it is."

"I said leave it alone!!" Maybe someday he will tell me what happened. Mama comes outside with her purse and bible in one hand and a couple of bowls in the other.

"Can you go get the pies off of the table?" she asks me.

"Sure." Olivia and Isabelle come outside and head for the truck. They are in a hurry to get to the truck so they won't have to carry anything. Mama stops them and hands them the bowls of food.

"Don't move so fast I need some help carrying this stuff." Well, they didn't get out of it after all!

"Yes, Ma'am." they say. I can't help but smile, they just weren't fast enough.

We all squeeze in, Mama turns the key and it rumbles to life. After letting it warm up for a bit, Mama puts in drive and we start down the road. Everyone is chattering and laughing, we're all in a really good mood. I guess it's the sunshine and the birds and just everything. We pass Bobby's house, his family is outside getting in their car for church. I wave at Bobby and he waves back.

"Aren't you sweet on Bobby?" Isabelle teases.

"No, it's not like that at all! We're just friends!" I don't know what gave her that idea. I just don't think that way about him. Olivia and Isabelle are giving each other these weird looks and giggling.

"Don't be teasing your sister, girls. You don't like it when she teases you. Just think about that the next time she says something to you." Mama scolds them.

"Okay, Mama." Olivia answers. "When that boy becomes your son-in-law I'm going to say I told you so!" She giggles more and I reach behind Isabelle and hit her in the back of the head. She glares at me for a second, then grins and sticks her tongue out at me. Sometimes she can be very aggravating.

We finally pull into the church parking lot. It takes a few minutes to find a parking space because there are a lot of people already here. The big tour bus for the singers is parked there too. I'm the first one out, then Isabelle. Olivia sets one leg out the door and then stops. Her face gets really red and I follow her gaze and discover what she is looking at. It's Charlie Turner, the preacher's son. Well, well, I think she just might have a crush on this guy. I'll have to file this away for future reference.

"Hey, Alex!" Bobby calls from the spot where they parked their car. I look around and spot him then wave.l look back at Mama and she just smiles and nods.

"Go on! Just be sure you listen to the sermon. I need you to take these pies and put them on the table first." By the time I have them picked up, Bobby is beside me.

"Good morning, Mrs. Stafford. How are you doing this morning?" he asks Mama.

"Good morning Bobby, I am doing just fine, how about you?"

"I'm doing okay. Good morning Alex."

"Good morning Bobby. Let's go take these pies to the table."

"Hi, Alex!" Carl yells as he runs toward us. He stops directly in front of me and gives me a big hug. I laugh and hug him back

"Hi, Carl! It's good to see you."

"Good morning, Mrs. Stafford." Carl says. Mama smiles and tells him good morning and gives him a quick hug. Carl is always smiling and he likes to hug people. He is very affectionate. We start toward the picnic tables they have set up under the big oak trees. They are loaded down with food.

"I've got something to ask you. My Aunt Theresa gave me a little Maltese dog, it's a house dog. Mama says I can't keep it because of Carl, she's afraid he might hurt it without meaning to, it's so small. You know how he likes to hug everything. Well, anyway, I was thinking that you might like to have it. Her name is Milly." Bobby asks me.

"I would love to! I'll have to ask Mama first, I'm sure she will let me have it." The service is starting so we quickly find a seat near the back row. Carl sits with us. When the singers get started, he claps his hands enthusiastically. He loves music. It tickles everyone to see him enjoy it so much. There is a lot of good singing and then the preacher gets started. He has a good message. After he's through, the singers come back for a few more songs. Finally it's lunch time.

"It's about time, I'm hungry!" Carl says. He just tells you like it is sometimes. Everyone files out the door and gathers around the tables of food. They were all laughing and having a good time. The small kids were running and playing. Olivia and Isabelle are standing with their friends,

Victoria and Hannah. They are giggling about something. Charlie walks past them and Olivia blushes and lowers her head. I just can't get over the fact that she is actually kind of shy. She is usually very outgoing. She must really like this guy.

Mama, Mrs. Buckner, and Mrs. Turner walk out the door. Mama on one side of Mrs. Buckner and Mrs. Turner on the other so she won't fall going down the stairs. I can't wait to ask her about the dog. I really hope she lets me have it. I spot Carl standing with Mr. Turner, smiling and shaking everyone's hand. His happiness and enthusiasum is contagious.

"Alex, can you help Mrs. Buckner find a seat? I'm going to help get the food ready." Mama asks as she goes toward the tables, where several other ladies are already taking lids off of bowls and uncovering platters.

"That's okay, honey, I think I can find a good seat." Mrs. Buckner speaks softly.

"I don't mind at all." I smile and take her arm and help her to a chair sitting under the tree. She is a very sweet lady.

"Thank you, my dear. You are a very considerate child. Your mother is lucky to have you."

"Do you want me to get you a plate? That way you don't have to get up and lose your chair."

"Are you sure you don't mind? I don't want you to miss out on anything for yourself."

"I don't mind at all! I'm glad to get it for you. What would you like?"

"Well, I would like a piece of fried chicken and the fixins to go with it. You know what I like. I'll trust your judgement." Bobby and I go to the tables to get her plate and take it back to her. Mama is standing at the end of one of the tables.

"Mama, I need to talk to you about something." I tell her.

"Sure, what is it?"

"Bobby's Aunt brought him a little dog and his mom won't let him keep it because she's afraid Carl will hurt it without meaning to it's so little. He was wondering if I wanted her."

"Oh. What kind of dog is it and is it housebroke or what?"

"Yea, it's a house dog and it is housebroke. She is a Maltese and her name is Milly."

"Has she been fixed?"

"I don't know. Bobby didn't say. I can find out, though. Let me take this plate to Mrs. Buckner and I'll ask him."

"Ask him what?" Bobby ask from behind me.

"Oh, I didn't know you were behind me. Mama wants to know if Milly has been fixed."

"Yea, she has been fixed. She's a year old. She also has papers with her."

"Papers aren't that important, especially since she's been fixed. Let me think about it and I'll let you know later. Take Mrs. Buckner her plate before she falls over from starvation." She smiles at us and motions for us to go on.

"Maybe she'll let me have her. I sure hope so." I tell Bobby as we deliver the plate and a drink to Mrs. Buckner.

"Thank you dear." Mrs. B. tells us as she gets her plate. We hurry back to the tables to fill our plates. After filling our plates, we find a nice shady spot under a tree where someone spread a blanket for people to use.

"This is really nice. It's good and cool here. Do you think that maybe your mom will let us all go swimming next week?" Bobby inquires.

"It would be really nice. It's supposed to get pretty hot next week. We need to go riding sometime soon, too. Star hasn't been exercised in a long time. I guess Ladybug hasn't either."

"No, she hasn't. I wish you would look at that!" I quickly look to where he was pointing. There stood my sister, Olivia, looking down at the ground and blushing while Charlie Turner was standing beside her and talking. She was actually blushing!! This is a sight that I will not be able to get out of my head for a long time to come. She's usually flirty and talkative with other people.

"Well, what about that!" was all I could say. We looked at each other and laughed. The rest of lunch goes pretty well.

After everyone is finshed eating, the food is all put away, and everyone is still visiting with each other, the band moves outside on the porch. They set up all their instruments and starts singing. It is really great. The sound of rejoicing fills the air. Several of the older ladies "Get happy" and shout and raise their hands in the air to praise God. There is a sense of peace and well being over everyone. There is just no way a Sunday afternoon can get any better. The singings lasts about an hour or so longer then they step down from the porch. We all mingle around and get ready to go home. There is a general exodus to the cars. Everyone waving and hugging and saying good bye for the day. It's been a very good day!

"Here comes your Mom. Ask her again about Milly." Bobby tells me when we get to our truck

"Hey, Mama. Let me help you carry that." I meet her halfway to the truck and take the bowls she is carrying.

"Be careful. I filled them with food for your Daddy."

"Okay, I will. Did you ever figure out if I can have Milly or not?"

"Well, just have two questions. Will you take care of her and feed her and give her all the love she needs and where are you going to get food to feed her?"

"I've thought about that You know I do work for Mrs. B. and she pays me. I can use that money to buy her food and yes, I will take care of her and give her all the love and care she needs."

"I think you will. I guess you can have her. We'll stop at the store on the way out of town and you can get her some food." I smile and kiss her cheek.

"I would hug you but I don't want to get food all down the front of your pretty dress!!"

"That's okay. Let's just pretend like you did!" She laughs and we walk on to the truck.

"I can have her! Can we pick her up on the way home from town?" I tell Bobby, excitedly.

"Sure, we're going straight home. I guess I'll see you then!" He waves as he walks to their car where his Mama and Daddy and Carl are waiting for him. Olivia and Isabelle climb into the truck next to Mama and I get in next to them. On the way out of town, we stop at the grocery store. I quickly go inside and find some dog food for Milly. When I come back out, my sisters are arguing about something. That's really not that unusual because they argue a lot. Mama says it comes with their age.

"I told you two to drop it! What I say goes and that's final!" Mama says as I get into the truck.

"But Mama, it's just a party for us kids. There's not going to be anything bad there." Olivia whines.

"I just don't like the idea of you going to someone's house when their parents are not home and they don't know that there's going to be a party. That's an invitation for something really bad happening. Anyway, these kids are too old for you. They're college kids and there will probably be drinking and I don't know what else there and you are not going! That's final!"

"I don't ever get to do anything! All I get to do is stay home and waste away!!" She whines again. There is a heavy silence the rest of the way home.

Bobby's house comes into sight. Mama start slowing down as we get close to his driveway. I can see Carl running around the yard. He probably ate too many brownies. He loves them. As we pull into the driveway, Mrs. Hall comes out of the house and calls for Carl to come inside and change out of his good church clothes. He laughs and waves at us and runs into the house. Bobby comes out with a small ball of white fur in his arms. The ball is wiggling and licking his face. I get out of the truck and meet him as he steps off the last step. He hands the ball of fur to me.

"This is Milly. She is very sweet!" Milly looks at me with big brown eyes and it's love at first sight. She studies me for a minute then wags her tail and licks my face.

"She is great!" I tell him, laughing. She continues to lick my face.

"She really likes you. I thought she would. She has very good taste!" He tells me."Are you sure you want her?" I think he already knows the answer to that.

"Of course I do! She is a sweetheart! I will take very good care of her and you can come see her anytime you want to."

"I know you will. I would rather you have her than anyone else I know."

"Thank you so much! I guess I'd better go. Daddy is probably wondering what happened to us. He's probably getting hungry by now, too." I walk back to the truck. Isabelle opens the door for me and reaches for Milly.

"She is so cute! What's her name?" she asks me. I hand Milly to her and get into the truck. Milly studies Isabelle and then licks her face, too. Olivia reaches over and pets her too. I think she is going to have a very good home. Bobby waves as we pull out and head home.

"Milly is her name. Bobby's aunt gave her to him and his mama said he can't keep her because she's afraid Carl will hurt her because she is so little. He wouldn't mean to hurt her but you know how he likes to hug everything and she is small." I tell them.

"Does she stay in the house?" Olivia asks.

"Yea, she is a house dog. Being outside all the time would probably kill her."

"What's Daddy going to say about it?" Isabelle asks.

"That's a good question. I don't know what he is going to say. I'll run interference for you." Mama comments. We pull into the yard and Daddy is sitting on the porch in his chair. His head is laying to one side so I guess he's asleep. When he hears the truck, he jerks his head up and looks around.

"It's about time you got home!" He says, hatefully. He's always a grouch when he first wakes up.

"I told you we would be gone just about all day. You knew there was a singing and dinner." Mama tells him.

"Did you bring me anything to eat?"

"Yea, we brought you a lot of different stuff. All the things you like." Mama tells him as she goes into the house.

"Well, bring me a plate!" he orders. "What have you got there?" he asks me as I walk up the steps.

"It's a house dog, her name is Milly."

"Where did you get her?"

"Bobby Hall gave her to me. She's a very sweet girl." I stand still waiting for him to say something.

"Make sure you take care of her!" was all he said. I guess I can keep her.

"Thank you, Daddy." I lean over and kiss him on the cheek. He smiles and pats my hand. Deep under all the gruffness, there is a good heart.

"What are you two up to?" he asks my sisters.

"Nothing. we're just going to go change our clothes." Olivia answers. They both lean over and kiss him on the cheek as they go by.

When I get to my room, I sit Milly on the floor and she explores the room. Not missing anything. I quickly change my clothes, hang up my dress, and put my shoes in their box on the shelf. Milly jumps on the bed and grabs a stuffed bear I have laying there. She looks at me and then shakes it and kind of growls deep in her throat. I laugh at her, she looks kind of funny because the bear is almost as big as she is. I guess she doesn't really care. She wags her tail, drops the bear and barks wanting me to play with her. I grab the bear and the fight is on. To be so little, she's pretty stout. We wrestle for the bear for a few minutes, then head to the kitchen where Mama is fixing Daddy's plate of food.

"Did you remember to bring in Milly's food?"

"No, I forgot. I'll go get it right now."

"Okay, then you can take your Daddy his plate and something to drink. I'm going to finish putting up this food in the fridge so it doesn't ruin, Somebody might want it later."

"Sure." I pick up his plate and go toward the front door. Milly right behind me. She does stop occasionally to check out a smell or investigate something that looks interesting to her. I make sure the front door doesn't close on her as she comes out right behind me.

"It's about time!" Daddy says. "I was about to dry up and blow away!" I hand the plate to him, along with the coke.

"Here you go, Daddy. Mama tried to get all the stuff that you liked." Milly is cautious as she comes down the steps after me. She slowly looks around the yard and smells of everything. I go to the truck and get her bag of dog food out of it. She gets excited and starts wagging her tail when I get back to the steps and start up them.

"She seems to like you already. She is awfully cute. Is that as big as she's going to get?" Daddy asks.

"Yea, she's full grown."

"I bet Bobby just gave her to you because he likes you." He says with a grin.

"Now, daddy. You know better than that! We've been friends for years."

32

"Okay, if you say so!" Why does everyone seem to be making a big deal about Bobby? I know they are just teasing, but it just seems that they are really making a big deal out of nothing. You know the saying, A mountain out of a molehill. Olivia and Isabelle come traipsing down the stairs and onto the porch.

"I noticed that you were getting awfully chummy with the preacher's son!" I tell Olivia hoping to get the subject off of me.

"I was not! We were just talking!" Her face turns red as she responds.

"Tell me more!" Daddy says between bites.

"They just seemed to spend an awful lot of time togethor today. I think Olivia was even blushing at one time!"

"Do tell!" Daddy says with a grin.

"Yea, she sure giggled a lot, too!" Isabelle decides to join us in teasing our oldest sister.

"Now, we are just friends!" Olivia stammers.I quickly make my exit to the kitchen with Milly in tow.

"You look like the cat that just got the milk. Whats going on?" Mama asks as I come into the room and sit the dog food on the floor next to the refrigerator.

"We were just teasing Olivia about Charlie.I told Daddy they were awfully chummy today."

"It's not very nice teasing your sister like that."

"They were teasing me! I was just getting the subject away from me!" Milly is waiting for me to pour her some food. "Do you have a bowl I can use for Milly's food and water?"

"Sure." she reaches into the top of a cabinet and hands me a couple of old dog bowls. I fill them up with food and water and sit them next to the garbage can so they will be out of the way. Milly checks them out and gets a drink of water. She turns around and wags her tail to say Thank you. About that time the phone rings. I can hear my sisters racing to see which one gets there first. Isabelle answers it and talks for just a minute then she takes the phone to Daddy. It's usually either for him or one of them. I hardly ever get any phone calls. Mama either as far as that goes.

The conversation isn't very long. I hear daddy mumbling something about having to go and he hangs up the phone. Mama and I go to the porch and sit down in the last two empty rocking chairs.

"Can you believe that?!!" He exclaims. "That brother of mine sure has a lot of nerve! Don't hear from him in nearly a year and out of the blue he calls wanting to get me to sell this farm!! He says we could make a lot of money now that the land around here is being developed and people from all over are coming in here and buying property because they want to get away from the city. It'll be a cold day in hades when I sell this place and I've told him that before!" He is really very upset.

"Calm down, Jim. You know this place is ours. He can't force you to do anything." Mama tells him, laying her hand on his leg.

"I know he can't. It's just the thought of it! He got what he wanted when Mama and Daddy died. He wanted the money so he took it and ran. Now he thinks he should have it all!"

It's really a long story about Daddy and his brother, Larry. After Grandma died, we moved in here to take care of Grandpa. Uncle Larry and Aunt Liz wanted to put him in a nursing home so they wouldn't have to take care of him. They said they didn't have time to look out for him. Daddy told them no way that we would move in here and take care of him ourselves. I barely remember moving here. I was pretty young, I hadn't started school yet. I can remember hanging out with Grandpa and he would teach me things about animals and raising a garden. We would go walking hand in hand to the barn and around the fields. His health started going downhill when I started school and he was sick for a long time. He died when I was 7. I really miss him. Anyway, he had changed his will. He left the farm and house to us and the money and things that were in the bank went to Uncle Larry and Aunt Liz. They were pretty mad because they didn't get it all. I don't know what made them think they would get it all. They sure wasn't here when Grandpa needed hetp getting up to go to the bathroom or when he couldn't sleep or when he just needed someone to talk to about Grandma and the old days. All they are concerned about is money and how much they can get and how much they can keep.

"I'm sorry, Jim, I don't understand them either. Your Daddy and Mama put their lives into building this farm. They raised their family here. Your Daddy built this house by himself. I just can't understand why that doesn't mean anything to them." Mama tells Daddy.

"It's because Larry doesn't have much of a heart! He lost what he had a long time ago! When he met that Liz, his whole attitude changed. She always had money and she wasn't going to do without it!" Daddy says.

"Now, that is not true. It takes two. I guess he just got tired of being poor and decided he wasn't going to be no matter what it took. He lost track of everything that really matters. His priorities are all wrong. Maybe he will see that they are someday and put them back right"

It takes a little while for Daddy to calm down. He gets really excited about things sometimes. I can't blame him. though. Grandpa and Grandma did work awfully hard on this farm and raising a family. Uncle Larry has always seemed to get things the easy way. I guess that's why Daddy is in the shape he's in and Uncle Larry is not. Milly runs around in the yard and chases leaves and twigs. Rufus doesn't know what to make of her. He just sits and watches her warily. I think he will eventually make friends with her.

We spend the rest of the day sitting on the porch and talking. Sometimes, we just sit quietiy and listen to all the sounds of nature. It's times like this that I will always remember. There doesn't seem to be any problems or stress right now. Its just us as a family, enjoying each other's company and the rest of the world doesn't really matter. Slowly, the sun sets and it starts getting cooler. This has got to be my favorite time of day. The frogs start croaking and somewhere off in the woods an owl hoots. It's kind of a lonely sound.

"I guess I'm going to bed now. I'm tired." Daddy says, as he gets out of his rocking chair. The squeiking sound startles Milly and she kind of jumps a little and looks toward the sound. She is sitting on my lap and I put my hands on her so she won't fall off.

"Good night, Daddy. I hope you feel better in the morning." Olivia tells him.

"Good night. We love you!" Isabelle tells him.

"I love you all, too." He answers and goes into the house. He heads toward his bedroom and shuts the door.

"Well, girls, I guess I'm going too. Don't you all stay up too late! There are a lot of chores to be done tomorrow. The garden needs working before it gets too hot" Mama says and starts into the house. Most of the stuff we can because the electricity is so undependable out here. My sisters don't like working in the garden, but they do it without too much of a fuss because they know Mama and Daddy will be very upset and they will be in big trouble if they don't. Plus, they get new school clothes out of the money we get. I like working in the garden. I love the smell of the fresh turned earth and the feel of it under my bare feet. Grandpa always said I was a born farmer. I guess I got it from him, after all, he's the one that taught me all about it.

"I'm going, too. I will see you all in the morning!" I scoop up Milly and we head toward our bedroom. She wanders around and inspects things as I get ready for bed. It's still pretty warm outside, so I leave my window open. The night sounds make a good lullaby. When I get into bed, Milly curls up beside my feet and makes herself comfortable. I reach down and pat her and close my eyes. I say a prayer, thanking God for all his blessings and thanking him for Milly and my family. A lot of the people around here don't think very much of us because we don't have a lot of money or a big fancy house or a fancy car. All they worry about is where their next hundred dollars is going to come from and what they have to do to get it. They call us lazy because Daddy and Mama don't work in one of the factories in town and make all kinds of money. They don't realize that we are the ones that are truly blessed. We don't have all the hassle and stress that other people have. The main thing is that Mama and Daddy are there for us. We are really happy. We have to depend on God to provide for us, after all, that's what the bible says to do, isn't it? We have never gone hungry or gone without the basics. That's all that really matters. We have a lot to be grateful for!

Chapter 4

The week started off pretty good. We were busy all day Monday working in the garden. Tuesday, we went to Mrs. B.'s and worked. I always get the job of mowing her yard. She always slips me a little extra, too. Wednesday, it rained and stormed all day. We worked in the house with Mama. She bakes homemade bread for one of the local country stores not far from here. It's kind of like a tourist attraction. People come from the city and want to spend time in the country. That's okay, as long as they spend their money, too. Mama also makes other things to sell. Her embroidered stuff sells pretty good, too. Not many people do that anymore. The city people think it's cute and quaint. She's always got something she works on with her hands. Either a quilt or pillow cases or something like that. She does it all the time. The only time I have ever seen Mama without something to do, was when she is sick. Which, thank God, isn't very often.

Thursday starts off like any other day, with all the chores getting done. After breakfast, the phone rings. Olivia rushes to answer it. "Alex, it's for you!" I can't believe it. I hardly ever get a phone call.

"Hello?" I answer.

"Hey! Whatcha doin?" Bobby's cheerful voice comes over the line.

"Hey! We just got finished with breakfast What are you doing?"

"Nothing much. Can you go for a ride today? I thought we could go to the blue hole." The blue hole is on the river not far from where we live. It's a good ride to get there. You can't get to it without a horse or a motorcycle or four wheeler. The reason it's called the blue hole is because it's pretty deep and the water looks blue all the time. Some of the local kids go there to swim. Not many people will go because it's so hard to get to.

"That sounds like a good idea. Star needs some exercise. I'll ask Mama and find out if she needs me today. Hang on just a minute." I lay the phone on the table then quickly walk to the kitchen where Mama is. "Bobby is on the phone and he wants to know if I can go riding with him today. Do you need me?"

"I guess I can do without you. I was just going to deliver this bread. Your sisters can go with me. I'm sure they would like a day off away from the house. Where are you two going?"

"We're going to the Blue Hole. Could you pack us a lunch or something? We will need some drinks, too."

"Yea, I guess I could fix you some lunch to take with you. Be sure you take your swimming stuff and a towel. I know you can't resist the water!" She knows me all too well!

"Thanks, Mama. I love you very much!" She just smiles and nods as I go back to the phone. Bobby and I make plans to meet in an hour or so and head out. After getting ready, with my bathing suit under my clothes, I go to the barn to get Star ready. When I approach the gate with his saddle in my hands, he perks up his head and prances over. He knows he's getting to go for a ride. He's kind of excited and it's hard to get him to stand still so I can put the saddle on him. Finally, it's done and I lead him back to the house, tying his reins to the porch rail. Mama comes out on the porch with the saddle bags filled with lunch and drinks. She always packs way too much, I think she doesn't want us going hungry. As I get the saddle bags lashed down, Bobby and Ladybug come prancing into the yard.

"Hey, Ladybug looks like she's ready to go for a ride, too. I know Star sure is!" I tell him.

"Yea, it took me a little while to get the saddle on. She is raring to go." I untie Star and swing into the saddle.

"Now you two had better be careful. Don't be gone all day. Be sure you get back before dark!"

"Okay, Mama. We will! See ya later!"

"Don't worry, Mrs. Stafford, I will take care of her. I promise!" Bobby tells her then we turn the horses and start down the road. There's a gate open in one of Daddy's hay fields and we take off through it. The hay is ready to be cut and Howard, our bus driver, is supposed to come tomorrow to cut it. He cuts everyone's hay around here. All he asks for is some of the hay to feed his animals. It all works out for the best for everyone. That's how good neighbors are with each other. The day is beautiful. The sky is the prettiest blue with not a cloud present. The birds are all singing and flying around looking for food. A rabbit scurries across the path in front of us. Somewhere in the distance, we can hear Rufus with his "I've got a rabbit!" bark. He likes to chase them.

"This is great! It is such a wonderful day!" Bobby says. "I bet the water will feel pretty good about the time we get there."

"Yea, it sure will. I'll race you to the end of the field!" I challange him and goose Star and off we go. He's only too willing to stretch his legs out and in just a heartbeat we're flying toward the end of the field, with Bobby and Ladybug in hot pursuit. It's a close race, a tie actually. We're both laughing when we get the horses stopped.

"That was a good race. It's about even!" I tell him.

"Yea, you got a head start or I would have beat you!"

"I don't think so! You're just slow on the uptake." We slow down and walk the rest of the way. There are a lot of trees and bushes and rocks along the path now. As we ride along, deep in conversation about everything in general, the sound of water rushing over rocks starts getting louder and louder. Pretty soon, the creek is running right along side the path. Several places we are able to see tiny minnows and tadpoles swimming. There are several good places along here to catch water dogs to go fishing with. We make good use of them, too. Up ahead, the creek widens considerably. The Blue Hole is just around the next bend.

"I don't hear anyone. Maybe we'll be the only ones here for a while." Bobby observes.

"It's still really early. A lot of people sleep late. I don't know how they do it, I can't sleep past 6:00 rnyself."

"Yea, but you are used to getting up with the chickens. Not everyone around here has to feed animals and take care of them like you do."

"This is true!" As we round the bend, we can see that there is noone here yet. There is a tree that hangs hallway over the water and it has a rope attached to it to swing on. It all looks so peaceful and quiet. We dismount and tie the horses to a large branch that is used for that purpose. There have been a lot of horses tied here over the years. The branch is even worn smooth from all the use. Bobby takes the blanket his mother packed for him out of his saddlebags and spreads it on the ground close to the water's edge. We both sit and listen to the water traveling over the rocks. It is such a peaceful sound.

"Look!" he takes my arm and points down the creek on the other side. He motions for me to stay quiet. A movement catches my eye. It's a deer walking cautiously to the water. When she reaches the edge, she looks around then looks back toward the edge of the woods. A very young baby wobbles out of the cover and joins his mother. They both dip their faces into the water and take a drink. The doe must have heard something because she raises her head suddenly and stands still, listening. The baby does the same. In a heartbeat, they both turn and sprint for the woods. It is such an awsome sight. I finally realize I have been holding my breath and let it out. Bobby is still sitting looking into the woods where they have disappeared. He looks over at me and jerks his hand away. He had been holding mine the whole time. He kind of turned red for a minute. "Wasn't that the most beautiful thing you have seen in a long time?" he asks.

"Yea. It was awesome! That baby was so cute." Now we can hear what spooked them off. Along the trail the opposite way we came was the sound of horses and people laughing. I guess our quiet time is over. I just hope it's some of our friends.

"Well, I guess somone else had the same idea we had." Bobby says. As we watch, several horses come into view. It's some of the older kids from school. We don't really know them very well, just who they are. They all ride up and dismount and tie their horses to the branch.

"Hi, guys. How's it going?" Eli asks.

"Okay, I guess. It's sure a nice day to go for a swim." Bobby answers.

"Yea, I guess it is. We're not bothering you, are we? We're just going to take a quick dip and then leave. We have to get back in time for practice this afternoon. The coach would kill us if we didn't show up!"

"Sure, no problem. You're not bothering us at all. We were just sitting here talking. Go right ahead." Bobby tells him. There are five of them, all guys. They are all from the football team.

"Olivia and Isabelle would love to be here right now! They don't know what they've missed!" I laugh and tell Bobby. All five have taken off their t-shirts and stripped down to shorts and now they are diving into the water. They are also very noisy.

"Yea, I can't wait to rub it in!" Bobby laughs too. We sit and watch them swim and jump from the rope. They are like a bunch of little kids goofing off and playing around. After about an hour or so, they decide to get out and get ready to go. When they are finally gone, everything is so quiet again, it's like a storm just left. It's our turn to get into the water, now.

"Last one in is a rotten egg!" I yell and head to the water. I know it's going to be cold, so I hold my breath and jump in before I can change my mind. If I stop to think about it, I won't ever get in. After getting in it's not so bad. I come up for air and Bobby surfaces beside me. Both of us laughing at the other one. We splash around and play for a while. When we finally get out, I guess it's probably around lunch time. We head back to the blanket with the towels Mama packed.

"Are you hungry?" I ask. "Mama packed some lunch for us."

"Sure. I could eat a bite." I get the stuff out of the saddle bags and we sit to eat and dry off. It won't take long to dry then we'll head back home. After eating, we put our trash back into the saddle bags to take home. The woods is not the place to leave garbage.

"I'm going to be gone next week. Remember, I told you I was going to my Grandmother's?" Bobby tells me.

"Yea, I remember. So, you're gong next week?"

"Dad gets off of work then and we're leaving Saturday morning and won't be back till the next Saturday." I feel kind of sad that he is leaving but I am happy for him to get to see his Grandmother. She's the only one he's got.

"I'll miss you but I hope you have a good time."

"I will. I'll call you, if that's okay."

"Sure, why wouldn't it be?" I ask him.

"I don't know. You sure your Mama and Daddy won't mind?"

"Sure, I'm sure. They don't mind when you call. They never have." After we get dried off, we put our other clothes back on, put the saddle bags back on, untie the horses and swing into the saddle. The trip back is a little sad because I know I won't see him for a week. By the time we get home it is late afternoon. Mama is sitting on the porch with Daddy.

"It sure took you long enough!" Daddy says. Sometimes I don't quite know how to take him because he sounds serious all the time. "Where did you go, China?" He laughs and I know he's just kidding around.

"Did you have a nice ride?" Mama asks.

"Yea, it was great! Everything went well." I tell her.

"Thank you for the lunch, Mrs. Stafford. It was really good. I guess I had better be getting back home. My Mama is going to send a search party out for me if I don't."

"Bye, Bobby and you are very welcome. I can't see you two go hungry!"

"I guess I will see you after next week. Have a good trip and enjoy spending time with your Grandmother." I tell him.

"Bye. I will call you." He turns Ladybug toward home and leaves, waving as he goes.

"I'm going to take Star to the barn and unsaddle him. I'll be back in a little bit." I tell Mama and Daddy. When I get to the barn, Puss runs in front of me, heading for the feed room. She doesn't even look around at all. That's not like her to act that way. Come to think of it, I haven't seen her at all for a couple of days now. After pulling up Star's saddle and brushing him down really good, I go into the feed room to get him a little treat. While I am getting out the scoop of feed, I can hear a little, high pitched sound. It only lasts for a second then quits. I stop and listen. It seems to be coming from the loft. After feeding Star, my curiousity gets the best of me and I climb the ladder to the loft. The sun has heated it up and the smell of hay is very strong. At the top of the ladder, I stop and listen. There is a scurrying sound and I follow it. There is a hole wallowed out in the hay and inside that little nest is Puss, with four of the cutest little kittens you have ever seen. She looks up at me and meows, as if to say, "What do you think of my babies?."

"So this is where you've been. What beautiful babies!" She starts purring and grooming the little ones as they snuggle closer to her. She is doing a very good job, seeing as this is her first litter. We didn't even know she was going to have any. I reach down and stroke her back. "Take care of these little fellows. They are very cute!" She looks up and smiles. Maybe not litterally, but I can tell she is smiling. I climb back down the ladder and go to the house.

"Guess what I just found?" I ask Mama and Daddy.

"I don't know, a pot of gold?" Daddy jokes.

"No, I found four of the prettiest babies you ever saw. Puss had kittens.!"

'Where did she have them at? I didn't know she was going to have any. She sure didn't look like it." Mama asks.

"They're in the loft of the barn. You'll have to be really careful when you put the hay in there." I tell Daddy.

"That's good to know. Howard is supposed to come cut tomorrow so we can get it in the barn about Saturday, Friday if we're lucky. It's not supposed to rain again till later next week. I guess you need to get everything ready for all the workers." Daddy tells Mama. She always fixes a meal and has water for them. It's the least we can do. She usually fixes stuff on the grill outside. Us girls help her all we can.

"Is Charlie coming to help this year? I'm sure Olivia will love that. She may even want to help." I ask.

"Now, Alex, what makes you say that?" Mama asks with a smile. I can tell she knows what I'm talking about.

"Oh, no reason!" I laugh. "Where are they anyway?"

"They rode their bikes down to the swimming hole. It should be about time for them to get back because I told them not to be gone too long." About the time she said that, we could hear them coming down the road, laughing about something. There is a swimming hole that is easy to get to about half a mile from our house. A lot of the kids go there on their bikes.

"Mama, guess what happened?!" Isabelle gushed excitedly as she pulled into the yard.

"No. let me tell!" Olivia interrupts.

"Anyway, There was a bunch of boys that were acting silly and trying to jump off the rocks. They were pushing each other and just acting like jerks. Anyway, Brad Anderson jumped off and didn't come back up..." Isabelle starts

"One of the ladies that was there with her little kids, jumped in after him and pulled him out of the water! He had hit his head on some rocks and it knocked him out. She had to do CPR on him till the rescue squad got there!" Olivia interrupts.

"We don't know who the lady was. Somebody said she was one of the new people that built a house on the property they developed. Anyway, the ambulance people said she saved his life. He almost drowned." Isabelle continues.

"Is he going to be ok?" Mama asks.

"I think so. They took him to the hospital to make sure." Olivia says.

"I know he had the biggest knot on his head I have ever seen!" Isabelle adds.

"Thank God there was someone there that knew what to do. I sure hope he's going to be okay." I tell them. Brad is a senior this year and on the basketball team. He's pretty good at it too.

"Those ambulance people really know what they're doing. Maybe that would be something one of you girls could get into. I hear they make pretty good money." Daddy comments.

"I don't think I could do something like that! I can't stand the sight of blood!" Isabelle says, with a shudder.

"They're called paramedics. It might be something to get into. That way I could help people." Olivia says. She was always wanting to help other people. Thats a good thing, if they want your help. She pretty much mothers everyone.

"Well, you two need to go put up your bikes. I'm not fixing supper tonight so there is some sandwich meat or leftovers in the fridge. Just be sure to clean up your messes." Mama tells us as she starts fanning herself with a newspaper she has in her hand. Milly jumps onto the porch and bounces into my lap.

"Hello, little girl. I hope you have been good today!" I scratch her right behind her ears and she wags her tail and licks my chin. "I love you too!" I tell her with a laugh.

"That dog is really something else! She got out in the yard playing with Ruftis today. You should have seen them! It was funny because he is about four times her size and she didn't back down from him a bit!! I think she's finally won him over." Daddy says. He must really like her, he doesn't get along with just any animal.

"I'm going to go take a shower. I smell like a horse!" I get up to go inside and Milly follows me and makes a beeline for her water bowl. I can hear her slurpping as I get some clean clothes to put on after my shower. She follows me into the bathroom and sits on the rug beside the bathtub, waiting patiently for me to get out of the shower. When I get out, my sisters are in the kitchen helping themselves to leftovers. Swimming works up an appetite. After the meal is over and the mess is cleaned up Olivia and Isabelle hit the shower, too. It's not long before it starts getting dark. We all make it to the front porch. This is my favorite time! We are sitting togethor and enjoying each other's company and the sounds of nature.

Chapter 5

A clap of thunder wakes me out of a sound sleep. Milly curls up against me even closer, shivering at the sound. I don't blame her, it kind of scared me, too. I look at the small alarm clock beside my bed and it says it is 6:00. There is a streak of lightning then another clap of thunder. This one rattles the whole house. The storm is getting closer and it sounds like it's going to be a doosey. I pull the quilt over me tighter and put my arms around Milly. I can hear Mama getting up and going into the kitchen. In just a few minutes, I can hear the sound of water running into the coffee pot. When it's full, the water shuts off and there's silence. Pretty soon, the aroma of freshly brewed coffee slips underneath the crack under my door as if to entice me to get out of bed. Usually it works, but this morning I just want to lay in bed a few extra minutes. All of a sudden there is a huge roar as the rain hits the roof. The sound is deafening because it's raining so hard. Suddenly, it gets louder and I can hear my sisters running down the stairs pretty quickly. Neither one of them likes storms too much. Mama opens my door and looks in.

"Good, you're awake. The news is giving severe storm warnings and they're telling everyone to be prepared to get to a place of safety. You'd better get up just in case." She tells me. She is afraid of storms because she was in a tornado when she was a kid. She is very protective about us.

"Sure, I'll get right up." I tell her as I swing my legs out of bed. Milly looks at me like she's not sure what to do. I follow Mama into the kitchen, where the radio is on and they're talking about the weather. The announcer is talking about a lot of hail and wind coming through the area.

About that time, the sound gets louder and you can tell there is hail hitting the roof.

"Oh, I sure hope it doesn't destroy the garden!" Mama says as she looks out the window. I do too. That's a lot of work. The wind is getting kind of rough. It's a good thing all the hay has already been cut and in the barn.

"According to the radio, the really bad part is going around us. I don't think it will hit here." Olivia says. "At least, I hope it don't."

"I'm sure it's going to be okay." Isabelle reassures her. Mama pours a cup of coffee and sits down at the table. Daddy comes into the room and sits in his chair.

"Boy, it sure is comeing a good one!" He says.

"Yea, it is. They're giving storm warnings on the radio." Mama tells him as she hands him the cup of coffee and gets up to get her another one.

"It ain't going to get that bad! It's not in a long time!" Daddy tells her. The announcer cuts into the music playing and says that the storm is just about over and they're lifting the warning. He says the storm just played itself out. "See, I told you. It always looses steam before it gets here! You worry for nothing, woman!"

"I can't help it! I would rather be safe and the girls all be safe!" She has a point. We all sit for a while with the rain hitting the roof the only sound. Milly jumps into my lap and curls up in a little ball. She's not worried.

"How about some breakfast?" Daddy asks, as the rain is subsiding.

"Yea, how about some pancakes?" Olivia asks

"I would like to have some gravy and biscuit!" chimes in Isabelle.

"I'll settle for a bowl of cereal myself." I voice my option.

"We'll have oats and sausage." Daddy settles it once and for all. Mama gets up and proceeds to make breakfast. Shortly the smell of frying sausage fills the air, lingering with the smell of fresh coffee. Outside the rain has just about quit

"After we get through eating, I think I will go out and look at the garden. Maybe it's not too bad." Daddy says as Mama sets a plate of sausage on the table. She spoons the oatmeal out of the pan into each bowl. By the time we have finished, the rain has completely stopped

There are even a few birds starting to sing. We help Mama clean up the dishes and Daddy goes outside.

"Did Bobby have a good time at his grandmother's? You never did tell us the details." Isabelle asks. It was sure a long week without him around. He called a couple of times but it's not the same as getting to see him.

"He had a very good visit. He loves seeing his grandma."

"I bet he got homesick! I bet he missed his girlfriend!" Olivia teases.

"Well, I am his friend and yes, I am a girl." I grin at her. "What about all these late night conversations with Charlie Turner? I would say it's getting pretty serious!" Her face turns the prettiest shade of red. "If you can't stand the heat, get out of the kitchen!" I whisper as I head out the door to do my chores. Milly tags along behind me. She will definitely need a bath by the time we get back to the house. All this rain, the dirt from the barn, and a little white dog is not a good combination. She frolicks along beside me, sniffing the flowers and jumping over a clump or two of grass along the way. She is having so much fun, I don't have the heart to send her back to the house. She's a lot of company, anyway. I would be really lost without her.

When I get back to the house, Daddy is sitting in the kitchen again. He is on the phone with someone. Mama is hovering over him and looking worried. I hope there's nothing bad going on. Olivia and Isabelle are sitting in the living room.

"What's going on?" I ask after making my way in and sitting on the couch.

"It's just Uncle Larry. I'm not sure what it's about but what I could gather before we were run out of the room, is that he has been to see a lawyer about taking this place and selling it." Olivia tells me, with a worried frown puckering her forehead.

"They can't do that! Grandpa left this place to us!" I tell her.

"Well, apparently, they're going to try." Isabelle says. She looks worried, too. We sit quietly, trying to hear what's going on in the kitchen. I don't know what we'll do if we lose this place. Daddy is not able to work and Mama can't either. Milly senses something is wrong and jumps into my lap and licks my chin. I hug her tight. The minutes drag by, all we can hear is the low sounds of conversation. We can't make out what's being said. The three of us are staring down at our feet, each one lost in her own thoughts.

"Girls, come here." Daddy finally calls for us. We get up and walk into the kitchen with a sense of dread. "I guess you know that was your Uncle Larry on the phone. I want to talk to you. This is very important and I need to know how you feel about it. After all, this is your home, too." Oh, no, here it comes. My stomach knots up and I feel kind of nauseaus. "He has been to see a lawyer about getting this place and selling it. He says he can do it, but I talked to the lawyer that handled the will and all the paperwork for your Grandpa. He says there is no way he can take it. The will is very plain about who gets what. We may have to sell some of the farm to pay for his services if it comes down to that. I need to know if you girls want to fight for this place or just sell it and give some of the money to Larry and take the rest and start over somewhere else."

"I don't want to lose the farm! This is our home! I don't see how he can take something that is not his.!" I tell him, matter of factly.

"I agree! This is home!" Olivia says.

"Me too. I wouldn't want to live anywhere else!" Isabelle agrees. Daddy looks at Mama. She smiles and lays her hand on his arm.

"Well, I guess that's settled! This is our home!" Daddy picks up the phone and dials some numbers.

"Mr. Smith? This is Jim Stafford. I just talked it over with my family and we have decided to fight to keep our home. We would like to have your services if you are available." He tells the lawyer. He listens intently for a couple of minutes. "Sure, I can deed you over a couple of acres of our property. We will be in to see you tomorrow, then. Thank you very much!" It's a good thing there are still people who are willing to help you without getting cash money up front. Hopefully, it won't come to this. Maybe Uncle Larry will see the light and this will be the end of it. I still can't believe he would do something like this. He is family, after all.

"Not to change the subject, but how was the garden?" I ask.

"It's okay, except for the corn. It kind of laid it over. It'll still be okay, though. It'll straighten back up." I'm glad to hear that. The phone rings, taking everyone by surprise. Mama answers it,. then hands it to me.

"Hello?"

"Good morning! how are you this beautiful morning?" Bobby's friendly voice comes from the other end.

"I'm glad you called." I take the phone to the front porch and sit in a rocking chair. I tell him about what's going on.

"I hate to hear that! Maybe you will still get to keep everything and not have to move. At least I hope you don't. I would miss you very much." Bobby answers. For the next hour or so, we talk about everything. Finally, Mama comes to the porch.

"Alex, I really need your help in the kitchen. It's bread day, remember? I've got some extra things to make. I have an order for cinnamon rolls." I love Mama's cinnamon rolls. They are absolutely the best!

"I've got to go so I can help Mama. Why don't you come over later. We're making cinnamon rolls and I know how you like them."

"Sure, I'll be there after lunch. There's some things I have to do here for Mama. She's wanting me to kind of keep an eye on Carl while she gets the shelves in the basement ready for all the canning she does." Carl hears his name and starts saying loudly, "Hi, Alex! I'm gonna have fun today!"

"I can hear him. Tell him I said Hi back and I hope he has a very good day today and has lots of fun!" I laugh and smile. Bobby tells him and Carl laughs excitedly.

"I'll see you later! Be sure you save me some cinnamon rolls!"

"Okay, I will. Talk to you later!"

The kitchen already smells like yeast. Mama is mixing the loaves of bread and sitting them on the shelf to let rise. My sisters are flipping flour at each other and laughing. Daddy finishes his coffee and sets his cup in the sink.

"I think I will walk the fences to see if a tree has fell on them." He tells Mama as he leans and kisses her cheek as he heads toward the door.

"Are you sure your back will take all the walking?" Mama asks.

"Yea, it feels pretty good today. I promise I won't overdo it" He lets the screen door slam as he goes out. When he wants to do some thinking, he takes off walking to be by himself. I know he's worried about his brother and the farm.

"Girls, quit wasting the flour!" Mama scolds Olivia and Isabelle. They look a sight with white flour all over their faces and in their hair.

"Yes, Mama!" They both giggle and flip one last bit of flour at each other. By the time the last loaf of bread is mixed and set aside to rise, the first one is ready to go into the oven. Pretty soon, the wonderful smell of fresh bread fills the whole house. The four of us stay busy and time seems to slip away. When the last loaf is finally in the oven and Mama is putting icing on the still barely warm rolls, there is a knock at the front door.

"Anyone here?" Bobby asks. He knows we're here. I guess he's just being polite.

"We're in the kitchen!" I tell him.

"You can sure smell all the good bread and those cinnamon rolls nearly to my house!" He exclaims as he walks into the kitchen. "I hope you saved one for me!"

"Of course we did. Don't we always make sure you get one?" Mama tells him with a smile.

"Pull up a chair and sit at the table. They're still a little warm, the way they're the best." I take a saucer down out of the cabinet and lay one on it for him. I go to the refrigerator and get a glass of cold milk and sit it beside the plate.

"Thank you very much. You make the best cinnamon rolls ever, Mrs. Stafford." That pleases Mama. She likes to see people enjoying the things she fixes. The phone rings and Olivia rushes to answer it.

"I'm getting a little worried about your Daddy. It's not like him to stay gone so long." Mama says, as she gazes out of the kitchen window. "I sure hope he's okay. I don't know whether to call someone or not"

"I'm sure he's okay. He has a lot on his mind." Isabelle reassures her.

"He's been gone a long time, though. It doesn't take this long to walk the fences to see about fallen trees." Mama replies.

"Mama, can you come here, please?" Olivia calls from the living room.

"What do you need?"

"I need to talk to you and ask you about something."

"Can't you come in here?"

"No, this is private and personal." Bobby and I look at each other with a puzzled expression. What could be so private that we all can't know about it? Mama lays the dish towel that she has been drying her hands with on the counter and walks quickly out of the room.

"Mama's right. Do you think we should go looking for Daddy?" Isabelle asks.

"Let's give him some more time. You know how he gets when he's really worried. If he's not back in a little while, we'll all get out and go hunting for him." I tell her.

"Do you think something happened to him?" Bobby asks, between bites.

"I hope not" was all I could think of to say. Mama comes strolling back into the kitchen with a smile.

"What's going on?" Isabelle asks.

"Nothing." She answers. That is most definitely not nothing, judging by the look on her face. Off in the distance, we can hear Rufus barking. Mama looks out the window and gives a sigh of relief "Here comes your Daddy. He looks like there's nothing wrong with him." I can tell she is relieved to see him.

"That's good. We were just talking about going searching for him." Isabelle says.

"I'm sure that wouldn't have been necesary. He can take care of himself." Mama replies. She was still worried about him, though. She stands and watches him cross the field to the house. Olivia rushes into the kitchen.

"Did someone say Daddy's coming?"

"Yea, he's walking across the field." I tell her. She grabs some old shoes that are sitting beside the door and slips them on, then she is out the door like a shot, heading toward Daddy. I wonder what that's all about. She sure is in an awful hurry to see him.

"Who was that on the phone?" Isabelle asks Mama.

"It was just Charlie."

"What were they talking about? It must have been important." I was fishing for information. Mama ignores my quiestion and just smiles to herself. This must be something!

"How about we go to the barn and do your chores a little early?" Bobby asks.

"All right. I guess Star wouldn't mind a little company. I want to show you the baby kittens, anyway. They are so cute We're going to have to find them homes before too long. They're just about old enough to wean."

"Thank you for the roll, Mrs. Stafford." He compliments as we go out the door. He is always very polite and Mama likes that

"You're very welcome!" Olivia is walking beside Daddy and they are deep in conversation. Bobby and I head to the barn.

"I wonder what's going on with Olivia and Charlie?" Bobby asks me.

"I was just thinking the same thing. It's about to kill me because I don't know." There is a small bark behind us and I look back. Milly is barrellling toward us, with her ears flopping.

"I can't believe her!" Laughs Bobby.

"She likes to go wherever I do. I think I would be lost without her."

"I was hoping she would have that kind of home. I was sure she would." The three of us walk to the barn. Milly spots Puss and the kittens. She stops for a second and watches them. They all watch her, warily. Puss finally decides she is harmless and continues sauntering around the barn, her kittens following. While we're there, we go ahead and do the feeding. Daddy always does the milking in the morning. We brush Star and talk about different things, mainly about the upcoming school year. its so hard to believe that summer is almost over with. With Star munching on his sweet feed, we head back to the house. It's starting to get late and Bobby has to get home.

"Mama will have plenty of supper ready if you want to stay and eat with us. I know she would be glad to have you." I tell him as we get to the front porch.

"I would love to stay but I already promised Mama I would get back before dark."

"Okay. Call me tomorrow, maybe we can go riding again or something."

"Sure. You know the fireworks display is coming up next week. Maybe you can go with us to see it."

"I'll ask Mama about it. I'm sure she won't mind. Let me know more about the details."

"I will. I'll see you later!" He starts up the driveway toward his house. Milly and I turn and go into our house. Everyone is in the kitchen. Mama and Daddy are talking about someone coming to visit.

"Now, Jim, you've got to give him a chance. After all, he is family. It wouldn't be christian to turn him away, now." Mama was saying.

"I know. All I can think of is that he's up to something. He's given me reason to think such things here lately!"

"What's going on?" I ask as we walk into the room.

"Uncle Larry is wanting to come visit." Olivia tells me. This can't be good.

"Why?" I ask.

"We don't know, honey. He just called your dad and asked if he could come see him." Mama tells me. I'm like Daddy. I wonder what he's up to.

"Is he bringing his whole family or what?" I ask. I'm not really thrilled with the prospect of seeing cousins I don't really know. They've always stayed away pretty much. I think Uncle Larry doesn't want to be reminded of where he came from or he doesn't want his family to know.

"I don't think so, he just wants to come talk to your Dad." Mama answers.

"I guess I can talk to him, that wouldn't hurt. I could see what he has to say."

"Okay, dear. Do you want to call him back tonight or wait till tomorrow?"

"I'll just wait till in the morning. Make him stew for a while." Mama finishes putting supper on the table. I wash my hands at the sink and sit in my normal place at the table. Isabelle keeps looking at Olivia and smiling.

"Have you heard the news, Alex?" she asks. Olivia looks down at her hands and concentrates on them.

"No, I haven't What's going on?" I am really curious.

"Well, Olivia has a date!" She grins. Olivia blushes and kicks Isabelle under the table.

"I told you not to tell!" She snarls visciously at her.

"Really? I can't believe it!" I tell them. I'm just surprised that it's taken this long.

"They're just going to church Sunday then out to dinner." Mama says. "I think it's very nice! Charlie is a nice boy." So that's what all the secrecy was about! He finally got up enough nerve to ask her out! Daddy must have agreed, too, or they wouldn't be going. I'm almost afraid to say anything about going to the fireworks with Bobby, now.

After the supper dishes are all done and cleared away, the phone rings and Daddy answers it. He goes to the front porch and sits in his chair. Mama sits in her chair in the living room and picks up her sewing. Of course, the other two go upstairs and listen to the radio. Milly and I go to our room and read a book. Pretty soon, it's dark and the house gets quiet. I am so engrossed in my book, that I actually don't hear when everyone else goes to bed. After a while, I fall asleep, too.

Chapter 6

Sunday finally comes, the day of Olivia's big date! She has been excited and nervous all week. I bet she has tried on every outfit in her closet at least twice. She finally settled on a pretty, powder blue dress. I really hope she has a good time. Daddy's brother, Larry, is coming here this afternoon. Actually, he is coming for dinner after church. He's bringing his whole family. He has three kids, two girls and one boy. They are Sara, 16, John, 14, and Rachel, 10. We are all kind of nervous about seeing them because we really don't know them very well. I think I have seen them maybe a couple of times. We all rush around getting ready for church. Daddy is even getting ready to go with us. Talk about a surprise! Ever since the day he took off walking, he's been different I don't know what happened, but I'm glad it did. He's like the old Daddy I remember from before he hurt his back. Charlie pulls up in his car and Isabelle spots him first.

"Olivia, your date is here!" She yells.

"Now, shush! I think she's had enough teasing this week, don't you?" Mama says. Isabelle just laughs and rushes into the bathroom as soon as Olivia comes out "You sure are pretty as a picture today!"

"Thank you, Mama." Olivia gives her a hug. Charlie comes to the door and knocks.

"Come on in, Charlie. I think she's just about ready to go." Mama tells him. He opens the door and steps warily into the house. Daddy comes out of his bedroom and walks up to him and shakes his hand.

"It's good to see you! You will be careful driving, won't you?" He says to Charlie.

"Yes, sir. It's good to see you, too. Are you going to church today?"

"Yea, I think I have been out long enough. It's time for me to get back where I belong." Olivia and Charlie head for the door. She stops and kisses Daddy on the cheek. "You two better get going. You don't want to be late. We'll be right behind you." They go out the door and Charlie opens the door for Olivia to get into the car. You just dont see many guys do that anymore. I can tell by the looks on Mama and Daddy's faces that they are impressed and pleased with the gesture.

"Well, girls, let's go! We don't want to be late, either." Mama tells us. We all pile into the old truck and head out to church. It sure is a beautiful day for it! I feel so happy as I look at Daddy driving and Mama seated close to him. He reaches over and puts his arm around her shoulders and gives a little squeeze. Mama smiles and lays her hand on his knee. Isabelle notices too and smiles. It seems like all is well with the world this morning. I just hope the whole day goes like this. Maybe Uncle Larry just wants to see Daddy because they are brothers. I sure hope so.

The church service goes very well. Bobby and Carl sit beside me. Of course, Carl is all smiles. He loves church. Everyone is glad to see Daddy. Just about everyone there comes to shake his hand and welcome him back. I can tell he's glad to be there, too. After the service, we all stand around and socialize just a little. Most of the men are talking about their crops and cows and the like. The women are all talking about their kids and grand kids.

"Come on, let's go outside where it's just a little cooler." Bobby says as he gets my arm.

"Right behind you!" I tell him. We go to the big shade tree beside the church. A lot of the younger people gather there. The conversation is about the fourth of July celebration and fireworks in town. There is usually a big cookout for the whole town, everyone brings something to contribute. It's really alot of fun. Mama and Daddy finally come out and look around for us girls. They motion for us to come on.

"I've got to go. We're expecting company for dinner and we've got to get back. Call me." I tell Bobby.

"Sure, maybe we can get togethor before the fourth. Good luck with today. I sure hope everything goes okay for you all." He knows all about the siruation with Uncle Larry.

"Bye, Alex. I will see you later!" Carl gives me a big hug. I hug him back.

All the way home, it's quiet. I guess we all have our own thoughts and it's about what the rest of the day is going to bring. When we get there, we all change our clothes. Milly is running around excitedly from room to room to make sure we're all there. She stops and looks at me when she can't find Olivia. "It's okay, Milly. Olivia has a date. Charlie is taking her out to lunch and they will be back in a little while." Milly wags her tail and jumps on the end of my bed, satisfied with my answer. She really surprises me at times with what she understands. She circles a couple of times and lays down. Mama comes out of her room and heads straight for the kitchen. Most of the dinner is already done, but there are a few things she waited till now to do. I think she wants it to be perfect. After I finish changing, I go to the kitchen to see if there is anything she wants me to do.

"Is there anything I can do to help?" I ask her.

"Me too." Isabelle says as she comes into the room.

"Well, you two can get all the dishes out and set the table. The good tablecloth is in the bottom drawer under the silverware drawer." She hardly ever puts the good tablecloth on the table. Only for special occasions. It was made by my grandmother Harvey. That's Mama's Mama. She died about three years ago. She was a very good lady. I didn't get to see her much because they live in Florida. Grandpa is still alive, but he's in very bad health and in a nursing home. Mama's sister, Trudy, takes care of him there.

"I'll get the tablecloth. You get the plates." Isabelle tells me. She spreads it on the table, the beautiful embroidered roses really stand out and add something to the table. I get down the good dishes, the ones with roses all over them, and set them the way they are supposed to go. Mama said that a friend of hers and Daddy's gave them that set of dishes when they got married. She was an older lady and she died of a heart attack several years ago. By the time we finish getting the table ready, we hear a vehicle pull up in front of the house. Mama looks at us kind of nervously.

"Well, girls, I guess this is it. I hope and pray everything goes okay." She lays down her dish towel and goes into the living room, where Daddy is sitting and reading the Sunday newspaper. Isabelle and I look at each other. We're both wondering about our cousins, since they are from the city, how different they will be. They come into the house. We can hear them all talking.

"Girls, come in here just a minute!" Daddy calls for us. We timidly walk to the living room. Uncle Larry and Aunt Liz are standing beside Mama and Daddy. Sara, John, and Rachel are standing just inside the door, looking around nervously. I guess they are worried just a little, too. Milly is bouncing around from person to person sniffing them to get to know them. Sara laughs and reaches down to pet her.

"She is a beautiful dog!" She pets her and Milly licks her hand. John and Rachel each gather around her to pet her, too. Milly seems to like them so I guess they are all right. You know what they say about a dog's judgement of character. It can't be beat.

"This is Alex and Isabelle. Olivia is not here right now because she has a date with a very nice young man for lunch." Daddy points to each of us and introduces us with a huge smile.

"They sure have grown! The last time I saw them, they were all a lot smaller." Aunt Liz says. "They are beautiful girls. These, of course, are our pride and joys. Sara, John, and Rachel." Everyone is smiling and the awkwardness is starting to wear off. Everyone finds a seat and there's a lot of catching up. Daddy and Uncle Larry are talking about their childhood and some of the things they used to do. From the sound of it, they used to be close.

"I guess everyone is hungry. Would you girls like to help get everything on the table?" Mama asks us.

"Is there something I can do to help?" Aunt Liz asks. "Sara, will you run out to the car and get the bowls and the cake I brought?" Sara gets out of her chair and goes outside.

"You didn't have to bring anything." Mama tells her.

"I know but I just thought it would be nice to bring a little something." Sara comes back in with a couple of covered bowls and a very pretty cake. We all head to the kitchen. Mama starts putting fried chicken on a platter and other things in bowls. She hands them to me and I put them on the table.

"This is a beautiful table cloth. Did you make it?" Aunt Liz asks Mama.

"No, it was my mother's. It was the last thing she made before she died." Mama takes the rolls out of the oven and puts them in a bowl. John comes in and grins.

"Boy, it sure smells good in here! I am about to starve to death!" He exclaims.

"You're always hungry!" Rachel tells him. He sticks his tongue out at her.

"Dinner is on the table. Isabelle, go tell your daddy and Uncle Larry to come on." She is the closest to the door and in a few seconds, she comes back with Daddy and Larry behind her.

"Would you like to say grace?" Daddy asks Uncle Larry. We all bow our heads while he asks the blessing. After he is finished, the kids all dig in first and go to the front porch while the adults all sit at the table. At first, things are quiet.

"What do you do for fun around here?" Sara finally asks. Isabelle starts telling her about all the things we do. It's not too bad, at all. They seem to be all right, just a little naive about some things. I would say we seem that way to them, too.

After dinner, we all help clean up the kitchen. Even John does his share. He kind of fusses about it being women's work but Aunt Liz puts a stop to that. After it's all done, we all go outside to the front porch. Daddy has to bring out some extra chairs to make sure everyone has a place to sit. In the distance, we can hear a car coming down the road. Charlie pulls in front of the house with Olivia. They both get out and walk to the porch. Olivia is laughing about something he said. She actually looks very happy.

"Did you two have a good time?" Daddy asks.

"Yea, we did. Thank you for letting me go, would it be okay if Charlie stays around for a while?"

"Sure, as long as his parents know where he's at and it's okay with them." Daddy answers.

"I already ask them if it would be okay and they said it would, sir." Charlie tells him.

"This is our oldest, Olivia, and her friend, Charlie Turner." Daddy introduces them to everyone. They all smile and say hello.

"You sure look like your grandmother." Aunt Liz tells her and introduces her clan.

"Alex, why don't you all show Sara, John and Rachel around the farm. I'm sure they would like to see all the animals and the barn." Daddy suggests.

"Sure, come on. We'll show you around." They all follow me to the barn. This is my territory out here.

"What beautiful kittens!" Rachel exclaims as she spots Puss and the babies.

"Do you like cats?" I ask.

"I love cats and other animals but we can't have them where we live. You are so lucky to be able to live like this. I hate the city!" She tells me.

"Yea, you really are lucky. We would love to live out like this!" John agrees.

"Come with me. You're not afraid of heights, are you?" I ask.

"No, we're not." They all agree.

"We're going to the hay loft. You can see for a long ways from up there. Just be careful." I look behind us, Charlie and Olivia are following at the end in their own little world, completely absorbed in each other. Lightning could strike all around them and I don't think they would notice. We all climb the ladder and make our way through the piles of hay to the window facing away from the house. There is a good view of the farm. "This is our farm. It's beautiful, isn't it?"

"Yea, it is!" Sara aknowledges. We just stand there in silence and admire the view. "I don't know why Daddy wanted to leave all this. I wouldn't want to." By the time we finish the tour, we have been gone a couple of hours, anyway. Our cousins are really not what we expected at all. They are really nice. I think we could get along with them very well, if we lived closer togethor. As we approach the house, we can hear the adults all laughing and talking. That's a good sign. At least they're not fighting. Hopefully, it's a good thing.

"What do you think about the farm, kids?" Uncle Larry asks his bunch.

"We think it's great! Can we come back to visit again?" Says John.

"I'm sure we can." Uncle Larry says. "I guess we'd better be going. It's still a long drive home. I will talk over your suggestion with my family and get back with you with an answer." He tells Daddy. They all say their good byes and get in their car and leave. After they are gone, we all sit down. Charlie and Olivia are standing under the tree in the front yard, next to the old tire swing. I guess he's saying his goodbyes. He turns and waves at us.

"Thanks, again, for letting Olivia come out with me. I would like to take her out again, sometime. You know the fourth is next week and everyone will be going to see the fireworks and to the picnic. Would you mind if I come get her and take her with me?"

"That would be fine, son. Be careful going home." Daddy tells him.

"Take care and be careful!" Mama tells him. Isabelle and I wave at him and he gets in his car and pulls out.

"Girls, I would like to talk to you about some things. Come here and sit down for a while." Daddy says. He sees the look on our faces and smiles. "It's not bad at all. I think you all will like it."

"It's a good thing." Mama adds. We all sit close togethor where we can hear him.

"I found out why Larry was wanting to sell this place. He has lost his job because the company he works for has downsized and he can't find anything else. He's been looking for a while now and there's just not anything. They are going to lose everything they have. I have suggested that he try to find something around here close and either build them a house or put a double wide or something like that on part of the farm. It's all paid for and they would have a place to live, after all, we are brothers and that's what Daddy and Mama would want. What do you think about the idea?"

"I think it's great! Sara, John and Rachel all said they would rather live out like this, anyway. What do you think they will do?" Isabelle says.

"I think it's great too. There's plenty of room here for all of us. They could go to school with us and we could show them around." I add.

"I don't know what they will do. You heard what Larry said about talking it over with the family and letting us know. I would hate to see them lose everything and have nowhere to go. That would be terrible and scary." Mama says. I guess we all shouldn't have worried about things today. At least we do have a home and will always have it. We need to be grateful for what we have. You can't judge what someone else does because you don't know the whole story behind their actions." Just then, the phone rings. Olivia rushes to answer it, even though Charlie hasn't had time to get home yet.

"It's for you, Alex! It's Bobby." She yells. I go inside and answer the phone. He wants to know everything that happened and I fill him in on all the details. He's happy that things went well, too. I guess we'll just have to wait and see what the future holds for us all.

Chapter 7

The fourth is finally here. Mama worked all day yesterday getting things ready to go. The Sheriffs Department blocks off all the streets around the square and the courthouse in the middle of town. Everyone sets up booths with all kinds of crafts and food. There are a lot of tourists that come to visit. Some of the local muscisions get togethor and put on concerts from a stage that the high school trades class put togethor. Mama and Daddy put up our booth yesterday and got it all ready. We have to take a few things this morning but most of it is already there. Daddy even surprised us by making a few wooden things, like some tables and a couple of very pretty cedar chests. There is also a beautiful gun cabinet with etched glass in it. That is what he was what he was up to all those times he left and didn't let us know where he was. He kept it all pretty quiet. He said it was a surprise for us. It sure was! He was working in Howard's shop and didn't tell us because he was afraid things wouldn't work out and he didn't want Mama to be disappointed again.

"Come on, girls. We've got to get out there early. People start shopping pretty early." Mama calls us from the kitchen. The smell of sausage and biscuits fills the air.

"We're coming!" Olivia yells from the bathroom. Isabelle rushes past my bedroom door on her way to the kitchen. Milly jumps off of the bed and follows her. I can hear Olivia coming out of the bathroom, so it's my turn now. Daddy is already in the kitchen, sitting at the table drinking his morning coffee. The rest of us join him.

"I hope you girls are ready for a big day, today!" Daddy says. "There's a lot of work to be done. Your Mama needs your help. We don't mind if you have fun with your friends, but be sure to help out, too. It's going to be busy and crowded." He taks a sip of his coffee.

"We know. It's always pretty busy." I tell him. We all eat our breakfast. The biscuits are really delicious today.

"Daddy, you do remember Charlie is comeing to get me this evening for the fireworks?" Olivia asks.

"Sure, he'll probably be around most of the day, anyway. He's supposed to help with the church booth for a while, isn't he?" he asks.

"Yea, I told him I would come help some, too."

"Thafs okay, as long as you still help your Mama and she says it's okay for you to go."

"Is Bobby coming to see you, Alex?" Isabelle asks.

"Yea. He'll be around most of the time. He's going to come help with our booth."

"You know, it's just not fair! Olivia has Charlie and you have Bobby and I have nobodyl" She pouts just a little. I kind of feel sorry, for her.

"Your time will come, dear." Mama tells her as she pats her on the shoulder.

"Don't worry about it too much. Your mama is right. Enjoy the time now. It passes soon enough." Daddy tells her.

It's about 5:30 when we finally head out toward town. It's going to be a beautiful day! The sun is already coming up and it's going to be hot After all it is July. There is a amall chance of rain showers this afternoon and evening. There is always that chance this time of year. I hope it doesn't spoil the fireworks.

"Did you bring the sunscreen?" Olivia asks Mama.

"Yea, it's in the bag in the back."

"Good, we'll need it today." We pass Bobby's house and they're not even stirring around yet. The factory where his dad works is shut down for the holiday so I guess they are taking advantage of that and sleeping in. When we get to town, there are a few people stirring around. Most of the early birds have booths and they're getting them ready for the day. The local diner is pretty busy. There are a lot of people eating breakfast.

Daddy pulls the truck to where our booth is and we unload all the things that Mama brought today. She starts uncovering the tables that have all her embroidered stuff and some more handwork. A couple of her quilts are hanging on some ropes stretched from a couple of trees in the corner of our area. They are very eye catching and beautiful. Several booths away, is Mrs. Phillips. She makes the best homemade doughnuts and she's got several tables full of them. Just about any kind you could ever want. That is the first place I am checking out First, we have to help Mama and Daddy get our booth ready. After everything is unloaded, Daddy takes the truck and parks it in the parking area. There are more people stirring around and getting things ready. Most of the people we know and they have all stopped and said hello and made a little small talk. It's nice being in a small town. In some ways and in some ways, it's not

"Here, Alex, I know you're wanting to hit Mrs. Phillips so go get us all some. You know what we all like." Mama tells me, handing me some money. I gladly take off to find some doughnuts. As you have probably guessed, that is one of my favorite foods. After picking out something everyone will like, I go back to the booth with arms loaded. Everyone gets the kind they like and sit in one of the chairs that we brought. Mama has thermoses full of coffee and several drinks in the cooler.

"I just passed somone that is making homemade ice cream! That will please Isabelle!" Daddy says as he saunters into our booth.

"Where at?" Isabelle asks, excitedly.

"I'll show you after while. They haven't even gotten started yet. You've got everything you need for now." He tells her with a smile. He knows how much she loves ice cream. He has been smiling a lot more lately. I'm glad he is happier.

"Hello, everyone! How are you all doing this beautiful morning?" Charlie's chipper salutation catches our attention.

"Good morning, Charlie. We are fine as frog hairl How about you this morning?" Daddy tells him.

"I'm okay, sir. I see you have gotten everything set up for the big day!"

"Yea, I hope it's going to be busy today so we can sell some of this stuff! That way we won't have to take it back home and unload it all."

Mama says. "Pull up a chair and have a seat for a while. Grab a doughnut and a drink." He walks around the tables and sits down next to Olivia.

"I really don't want a doughnut right now, thank you, anyway." He is always so polite. That's a big point in his favor with Mama and Daddy. There are several customers browsing around now. A lady stops and asks Mama about one of her quilts. From that point on, it gets pretty busy with lots of people coming through. After a while, Olivia and Charlie go off to the church booth to help out there for a while. Isabelle is waiting on customers and Daddy is talking to several people about his woodwork. I think he is even taking a few orders.

"You look like you're pretty busy. Are you too busy to go walking around with me to see what else there is?" Bobby's gentle voice asks from the corner of one of the tables.

"HI! Yea, we've been pretty busy, you know how it gets. I'll ask Mama if she can do without me for a while." I turn around and look at Mama and she motions for me to go on.

"Don't be gone too long! Be good, too." She smiles. Bobby and I stroll along the lines of table set up with all kinds of little knick knacks and food. We come across several friends from school and stop to talk.

"What would you like for lunch?" Bobby asks.

"I don't know. I'll have to go get some money from Mama and Daddy."

"No, I'm buying, what would you like?" That's really very nice of him.

"It really doesn't matter to me. What would you like?"

"How about one of those polish sausages with peppers and onions on it?"

"That sounds like a winner to me!" We get our lunch and walk leisurely around the rest of the booths and displays. When we get back to our booth, we're ready to sit down for a while.

"Well, it sure looks like you've been pretty busy." I tell mama.

"Yea, we've sold a lot of things and your Daddy has several orders for some of his woodworking projects."

"I still can't believe I have sold any of them. I just started doing it as something to take my mind off of some things and maybe be a little creative. Instead, I have found something I might be able to make a little money at." He was very pleased. I'm glad things are going a lot better for him. The afternoon goes by in a blur. There are a lot of people out this year. By the time the crowd starts dwindling down, we have sold most of the things we brought. There was a sweet lady from out of town bought two of Mama's quilts, she said she was giving them to her daughters for Christmas. She just kept going on and on about what a good job Mama had done on making them. Mama was just a little embarrassed. She doesn't take compliments very well. Isabelle finally went off with some of her friends for a little while. They wandered around looking at all the booths and socializing with other friends.

As evening came on and it started cooling off some, we started packing things up to put in the truck. Olivia and Charlie showed up to help and Isabelle came back. Bobby stayed to help, too. His Mama and Daddy had left and took Carl home for a while earlier because he gets tired easily. He wants to come back to see the fireworks. I like to watch him, his eyes always wide with wonder like he's just seeing them for the first time. It makes me and everyone around him enjoy them more. The boxes are all packed and the tables are folded and waiting for Daddy to get the truck and put them in the back. In the distance we can hear the old truck. He gets closer and closer and pulls up to the front of where our booth was and we all load everything that is left. Most of the people around us have already loaded and left so we have plenty of room to get the boxes put in the back just right. There are a lot less than what we came with.

"I bet you all are hungry! How about going to the diner and getting supper?" Daddy asks as we finish with the last box.

"Yea, we would love to!" Mama tells him. We don't get to eat out very often, just on very special occasions. Daddy takes the truck back to the parking lot and we all walk to the diner. It's full so we have to wait for a few minutes while they clear off a table for us. We finally get a table close to the window. The waitress brings our menues and we order. The conversation is all about the days' events and what a good day it's been. We linger over our food and enjoy the conversation. It's starting to get dusky when we finish. The sheriff's Department sets up the display in the large field at the edge of town, next to the park. There is a baseball diamond, some basketball goals, and a new soccer field there. We were all glad to get the soccer field. I think they may be starting a soccer team at school next year. The play area of the park is filled with trees for shade and all kinds of equipment for the smaller kids. There are also some picnic tables, a couple of shelters for parties, and some grills made out of rock. At the edge of the park area, there is a volleyball court filled with sand. All in all, it's a nice park and a good place to come with the family. As it gets darker, Daddy suggests that we had better get on over to get a good seat. I would say he's right, judging by the traffic already headed that way.

"Why don't Alex and Bobby ride with us?" asks Charlie.

"Sure, that way there'll be more room in the truck." I tell Daddy.

"Okay, just be careful and we'll see you there." He tells us. We climb into the back seat of Charlie's car and drive the short distance to the park. It is already getting pretty crowded but we manage to find a good spot to be able to see everything clearly. Mama lays a blanket on the ground for us to sit on and Daddy brings a couple of chairs for them. Daddy can't get down on the ground then get back up again because of physical limitations. Mr. and Mrs. Hall, and Carl find us and they set up their chairs. Carl plops down on the ground with us. His face is full of excitement.

"How are you doing, Jim?" Mr. Hall asks Daddy as they strike up a conversation. Mama and Mrs. Hall are lost in conversaton, too.

"I can't wait, can you, Alex?" Carl asks.

"No, Carl, I can't. It's going to be so pretty, isn't it?"

"Yea, I like all the pretty colors! Look Isabelle, there is a bug on the blanket!" His attention turns to Isabelle and the bug.

"Alex, this has been a really nice day! I'm glad we could spend it togethor." Bobby whispers in my ear.

"Me too." All of a sudden, there is a hush that spreads over the crowd. In the distance there is a large flash of light and some bottle rockets explode in the sky with brilliant yellow and red.

"OOOHHH! How pretty!" Carl exclaims, clapping his hands. For the next thirty minutes or so, we are all enthralled by the exploding colors in the sky and the loud booms. It's so magical. When the final burst of color slowly fades, the crowd begins to clap to show it's appreciation. Slowly, everyone gathers up their things and starts for their cars and the ride home after a fun filled day.

"Dad, do you mind if I ride home with Charlie, Olivia and Alex? We'll probably be right behind you." Bobby asks.

"No, I don't mind at all. Are you sure it's okay with Charlie?"

"Yes, sir. It's fine with me. I'm taking Alex and Olivia home, anyway. We're going right by there."

"Okay, then. We'll see you there." On the way home, Charlie is playing the radio. We are all pretty tired, so it's kind of quiet A good kind of quiet. It's been a long day.

Chapter 8

A couple days later, Uncle Larry calls. Daddy talks to him for a long time. After he gets off the phone, he comes into the kitchen where we're working on making some dill pickles to can. Mama is outside making sure there is a good enough fire in the wood stove and that the canner full of water is getting hot enough. We already have several jars full and ready to be put on the stove.

"What did Uncle Larry want?" I ask.

"We were just talking about my offer. Wait till your mama gets in here and I'll tell you the rest." Olivia is chopping up onions for a pot of garden soup later and she sniffles just a little. Daddy laughs and tells her it's nothing to cry about.

"Oh, you know I'm not crying! I'm chopping onions." Mama comes into the kitchen, wiping sweat off her forehead with a towel she has in her hand. It is pretty hot today!

"What did Larry have to say?" she asks Daddy.

'Well, he has decided to take us up on our offer. He is wanting to move here on the farm with us. They are in the process of selling their house and a few other things. With the money they're getting for that, they are getting a pre-manufactured double wide home and sitting it here. He is coming out tomorrow to go over the plans with me and decide where would be the best place to put it. He even has a job interview at the factory in town tomorrow. They are needing a new plant manager." He tells us. I can tell he's kind of pleased about it. I know it's what Grandpa and Grandma would have wanted.

"Well, I guess that means we're going to have new neighbors!" Mama says.

"Yea, Maybe we can have new friends, too. Even though they are family." Isabelle says.

"I'm glad, Daddy. After all they are family and family comes first!" I tell him. The farm is plenty big enough for all of us.

"Where do you think they will put their home?" Olivia asks.

"I don't know for sure. There is a nice place on the other side of the road across from the hay field. In fact, Larry always liked that spot and used to say he wanted to put a house there some day. I guess he'll get his chance." I know the place he is talking about and It is a pretty place for a house. Mama picks up the aluminum dishpan with the jars of pickles in it to be put in the canner and goes out the door.

The rest of the day is pretty busy. By the end of the day, we have about twenty five quarts of picles that are cooling on the picnic table outside. We are all very tired and looking forward to going to bed. The next week is very hectic. There are more vegetables out of the garden that need to be canned and the like. uncle Larry, comes and they decide where they are putting their home. It's going to be different having them so close. It's going to take about a month before they can move in, just about the time school starts. It passes pretty quickly, our days are filled with working on canning, working for Mrs. Buckner, and swimming and horseback riding. Gotta have some fun in there somewhere. The people come to clear off a spot for Uncle Larry's home with bulldozers and the like. It just takes them a couple of days to get it ready for some more people to come in and pour concrete footers for the trailer. It's interesting watching them. The day they bring the home is a scorcher. I believe it got up to one hundred degrees! It may not have but it sure feels like it. It doesn't take them long to get it all put togethor and set up. Next, there is a septic tank dug and the water system hooked up so they can have water. There is a city water line that runs out here but we don't have it. Daddy says it costs too much. Well water is better, anyway. Then comes the electrician. When that all gets done, it's ready to move into. By that time, it's only a week till school starts. I can't believe the summer is about over with.

Moving day dawns bright and clear. I rush to get all my chores done and breakfast ate. We are all going to help. The moving van is supposed to be there at about 7:00 this morning. After we all finish eating and Milly is put in my room for the day, which she doesn't much like, we head up the road to their new home. The moving van is already there. Charlie and Bobby come down the road in Charlie's car. They're coming to help, too. Everyone is busy all day, carrying in boxes and furniture. Aunt Liz is giving directions as to what box or piece of furniture goes where. It's tiring work and by the time we're finished, we're all ready for a rest.

"I've got supper at the house for everyone." Mama tells us. There is a line of tired people that goes down the road to our house. At least it's all done. Uncle Larry is going to take the moving van back to the rental place tomorrow. They'll be spending the first night in a new home. Every bite of food Mama has fixed is quickly devoured.

The kitchen is cleaned up and everyone clear out, going to find their beds. Myself included. The next week is spent doing normal things and helping our cousins get settled in. We even take them to the swimming hole and introduce them to all our friends. It's going to be different around here. Oh, and Charlie asked Olivia to go steady with him and even gave her a friendship ring. It's really pretty. They are nearly inseperable. Mama cried when she found out and saw the ring. I don't know why she cried, but I think it may have something to do with the fact that Olivia is not a little girl anymore. I think she might feel a little old. Daddy really likes Charlie, which is a very good thing. He has also started building a workshop beside the house for his woodworking. I'm glad he found something he likes to do. He's happier than I have seen him in a long time. He's going to church with us regulary and even insists on bible reading before we go to bed, just like he did when we were all a lot smaller. Uncle Larry, has been helping him. They seem to be getting along better. We are all glad of that.

Chapter 9

Get up, girls. You've got to go to school today!" The dreaded words. We all get around and put on new clothes and shoes and get ready for school. I sure hope this year goes well. Mama has breakfast ready and we wolf down sausage and biscuits.

"You had better hurry, I can hear the bus coming down the road!" Daddy yells from the front porch. We all scurry to the door and go outside, Milly sits at the door and whines, wanting to gowith me.

"You can't go to school, Milly. I'll be home this afternoon. You be a good girl today." I tell her. She wags her tail and jumps on my leg. I reach down and pet her on the head. The bus pulls in front of the house and we all start out to get on it Milly sits on the porch and watches us go, tail wagging.

"Bye. You all have a great day! I love you!" Mama tells us.

"Bye, girls, I love you, too. I'll see you this afternoon! Don't get into trouble!" Daddy laughs. He stands on the porch beside Mama and puts his arm around her shoulders.

"Good Morning, girls. I sure hope you all had a good summer!" Howard tells us as we step onto the bus. It still smells the same as it did last year.

"We did. We hope your summer was good, too." Olivia says.

'We have some new neighbors. They're our cousins. They will be going to school, too." Isabelle tells him.

"I know. I see that." We all sit down and he turns around and heads back the way he came. He stops and picks up Sara, John and Rachel. They are nervous and excited about starting in a new school. Uncle Larry is pulling out of the driveway, headed to work. He got the job at the factory and today is his first day, too. The bus doors close and we continue up the road to Bobby's house. Carl is outside on the porch waving. We all wave back. Bobby sits beside me.

"Well, it's back to school we go. It's going to be different this year." He tells me. Yea, it's going to be different We have all changed just a little over the summer. I guess you could say we have grown up some. There are a lot of things that have happened and we'll never be the same as before. I look around at everything and realize there is so much to look forward to. It's going to be a good year, I just know it!